ADRIFT

ADRIFT

Para H

ZORBA BOOKS

ZORBA BOOKS

Publishing Services in India by Zorba Books, 2019

Website: www.zorbabooks.com
Email: info@zorbabooks.com

Copyright © Para H

Printbook ISBN 978-93-88497-69-5
E-Book ISBN 978-93-88497-70-1

Zorba Books Pvt. Ltd.(opc)
Gurgaon, INDIA

To my wife, Shaku, and my IIT classmates,
who believed in me and encouraged me to
take this first, faltering, baby step.

CHAPTER 1

*W*hen Kate felt the first rumblings she was out on the balcony. She had been gazing distractedly at the hazy blue of the Southern California coast, sipping her coffee and thinking about the bombshell Peter had dropped on her that morning.

"Oh God! Not another one," she thought, as she reached instinctively for the railings. She had been through many of them in her 27 years in LA, so this didn't particularly bother her. She continued to sip her coffee unhurriedly. But, when she turned around, through the transparent patio door she could see the people inside scrambling about excitedly. George, the senior partner, had come running out of his office, looking worried.

"Maybe this one is a 5.6 or a 5.8. Perhaps more than a 6," she thought. She could still feel the rumblings. She knew from her professional training that the balcony wasn't the safest place to be during an earthquake, however minor. Moreover, she had to calm her staff down and get them back to their desks. She headed for the patio door, determined to take control of the chaos inside.

As she stepped back in, she heard the emergency signal trailing away on the secretary's radio. The announcer's voice came on. Somebody turned the volume up and suddenly there was a hush in the large room. Everyone was straining to hear.

"This is an emergency warning," said the announcer. "We are experiencing a major earthquake in the Southern California region. All citizens are advised to take shelter in the basements or go to the nearest emergency shelter. Please stay off the roads and await further details. The nature and extent of the damage is not clear at this time. We will update you with further information as soon as it becomes available."

The announcer's voice had no hint of panic. But Kate knew that didn't mean much. The announcers were trained not to convey their emotions. Also, they usually did not fully comprehend what they were reading out.

"Where the hell were you Kate?" George had sighted her. He walked across the room to her and quickly pulled her into his office, away from the milling crowds. "Just got a call from Paul. This looks bad. He heard from someone at the Seismological Institute. They think this is big. At least 6.5. The funny thing is they have no idea what's going on." Paul was the President of the company. "All their monitoring instruments are going crazy," George continued. "Paul's contact says he has never seen anything like this, including the big one in 92."

This worried Kate. "The big one" was the earthquake that tore up the Santa Monica Freeway in 92, destroyed half of LA and left several hundred people dead. But that had felt different. From the very first moment Kate had known it was going to be bad. She found it hard to believe the faint tremors she had felt out on the balcony could be anywhere near as bad as the 92 earthquake.

But what you felt could be highly misleading. It all depended on how far away from the epicenter you were. She suddenly realized she had no idea where the epicenter was.

"George, where's the earthquake centered?" she asked.

"That's one of the funny things. They have no idea. As far as they can tell, the entire landmass under Southern California seems to be shifting about. Their instruments cannot locate any epicenter. It sort of seems to be spread uniformly over the entire area. This guy over at the Institute was even talking about the possibility of a totally new seismological phenomenon."

"What do you mean a new seismological phenomenon? There is no such thing," Kate almost shouted without attempting to conceal her anxiety.

"Kate, think for a minute. What did you learn in your Geology courses back in school? A whole slew of contradictory theories about continental drift and plate tectonics. What do we really know about the earth's interior? We don't even have a good handle on how mountains and oceans are formed."

George was right, of course. And Kate knew it too. Geology, and what was really a specialized branch of it, Seismology, were relatively nascent fields of scientific endeavor. Much more was known about the far reaches of the outer space and the tiniest of subatomic particles, than was known about the mechanics of the earth's inner structure. How the continental landmasses, the oceans, and the mountains were formed and how they came to be the way they are, was largely speculative. So anything was possible.

"Jesus Christ! An unknown seismological phenomenon. And just about in the most vulnerable part of the U.S. That's the last thing we need. We've barely recovered from the 92 earthquake, and now this. This is not the time for new theories George," Kate was now visibly worried.

Just then they felt the entire building shake. Within seconds the shaking had become violent. The draws from the large mahogany desk in George's office came darting out and the wardrobe doors flung open with a loud noise. They could hear screams and the sound of people running about. The lights went out for a second and came back on. The emergency generator had turned on.

Without a word George and Kate rushed out of the office. The scene in the main room was unbelievable. Desks, draws, tablelamps and drawing boards were strewn about. The twenty odd people who worked there had run towards the exit and then stopped in indecision. They all looked scared. Some were near hysterical. Without realizing, both George and Kate had stopped abruptly right in the middle of the room, taken in by the devastation around them. Kate was the first to snap out of it.

"George!" she said, pointing to the people crowding near the exit, "we've got to get them to the basement. It may not be safe outside. Who knows what the hell this thing is about?"

"You are right Kate. Why don't you take them to the basement? I'll get some stuff... a flashlight, first aid kit, some crackers and cookies from the coffee room, and come right down."

"But we have all that in the basement George," Kate reminded him.

Their office building was brand new. Built after the 92 earthquake. Reinforced construction supposedly capable of withstanding even an 8.0. Most importantly, it had a basement designed to serve as an emergency shelter. It had its own store of dry and canned foods, juices, drinking water, blankets, beds and other amenities.

4

"Who knows what condition it is in?" said George looking embarrassed. It was his job, as head of that department, to ensure the emergency shelter was fully equipped with all the provisions. For about a year after the 92 earthquake, every couple of months they even had earthquake drills. But as the memory of "the big one" faded and the workload, fed by the economic boom, increased, the frequency of the drills decreased. In fact, they hadn't had one in the past three years and no one had even checked on the basement in at least two. All this had flashed quickly by in George's mind. "You go on Kate, I'll join you all in no time," he said and rushed back to his office.

The building was swaying now. "Part of the new earthquake-proof, flexible design," Kate thought, it was working exactly as it was supposed to. She walked in measured steps toward the exit, trying to look calm and self-assured. A faint smile crossed her face as she was reminded of her nickname. Calamity Kate, she was called. Not directly, of course. But discreetly, in whispered tones, behind her back. For her supposedly phlegmatic calm in crises situations. For stepping in and taking over bungled designs, slipping schedules, a project in disarray because of a chief architect lured away by a competitor, and any of a myriad other things that could go wrong. "OK Kate," she said to herself mentally, "let's see if you really are Calamity Kate or Catatonic Kate."

"All right folks, let's head for the basement. I think that's the safest place for us now until this passes over," she said addressing the crowd with a nonchalant sweep of her hand as though calm would be restored in a matter of moments.

The crowd followed her meekly, as crowds tend to do in such situations when instructed by an authority figure.

Kate turned the basement lights on and went down the steps with the crowd behind her. George needn't have bothered. The basement was spic and span and fully equipped. The janitor must have been cleaning the basement regularly. Kate made a mental note to give him a raise. It was just the kind of work ethic and attention to detail that pleased her. There was nothing much else that could be done. The crowd settled down, their varying degrees of panic temporarily in check. They could not feel the swaying here, but the reverberations from the ground underneath were much more palpable.

There was silence for a while and then people began talking in hushed tones. Various accounts of what they saw and heard emerged. Inevitable comparisons with "the big one" followed. Soon the crowd was split into two camps. One side held that the present earthquake - for that's what the crowd had assumed it to be and Kate had not shared the misgivings of the man from the Institute with them – was nothing much compared with the 92 earthquake. The other side argued vehemently that this appeared stronger and stranger.

Kate did not join in the discussion. She remained aloof. Ironically, the temporary calm had triggered thoughts of her own personal turmoil in her. She had stormed out of her house that morning, barely in control of her own senses. The most unspeakable and humiliating experience of her life, the kind that she always thought only happened to gullible housewives -not to attractive and intelligent professionals like her, had left her hurt, shocked and dazed. She had gone through extreme emotional oscillations ranging from all encompassing rage to an utter lack of any feeling, since early that morning when Peter had told her he wanted a divorce.

There had been no hints - no tiffs other than the regulation fights between married couples, no smell of unfamiliar perfumes, no tell-tale lipstick smudges, nothing. She had known Peter for seven years now, through two years of graduate school and five years of marriage. She had loved him intensely, liked him as a friend, respected him as a professional, and admired his intelligence and sense of humor.

Peter had tried to explain that it had nothing to do with any problem with Kate. He still liked her a lot. It was just that his interests had diverged from hers. What had brought them together was their passion for architecture and now he no longer cared for it. He had developed a new interest in Shakespearean literature. He had met a Chinese woman at work, had known her for two years. All the weekends Kate had thought Peter had spent huddled over his desk putting in extra time on the airport design project had actually been spent in the company of the Chinese woman attending the local Shakespearean productions. They both had made up their minds to resign and go back to school to study Shakespeare's works. He had told her all this calmly, rationally, pleading for her understanding and forgiveness. The more he begged, the more enraged she had become. She had thrown everything she could lay her hands on at him, including the kitchen knives. Fortunately, she had missed most of the time. Finally, weak and spent, tears still streaming down her face, she had walked out of her house and driven away, slamming the car door on Peter. Peter apparently cared enough about her to call the police and persuade them to track her down and stop her, thinking she might do something rash and foolish. So when a cop in a car with flashing lights had stopped and questioned her, Kate who had by then recovered some of her equanimity, had felt a mad rage again.

"Why can't the lousy son of a bitch leave me alone? Let him go consort with his Chinese concubine. Tell him I'll sue his bloody ass if he comes near me again," she had shouted at the officer who had gone back to his car thinking it was easier to handle race riots than domestic disputes.

Now, sitting in the basement, thinking about all this, Kate was overtaken by feelings of anger and sadness. But for the people around her, who viewed her as "Calamity Kate," she might have broken out in sobs of despair. She managed to check her emotions and continued with her musings. What had made this whole thing with Peter particularly hard was the memories of childhood it had triggered. A philandering father had ruined their family. He had not only blown all their savings, he had walked out on them - his wife and four daughters. Her poor mother who had never worked, except on summer jobs as a teenager, and was not particularly qualified to do anything, had been forced to take two jobs as a waitress. A day job from 7-to-2 and a night job from 5-to-12, leaving precious little time for other men or her daughters. This had left her hard and bitter and she had taken it out on her daughters. Mainly to escape their mother's inattention bordering on cruelty, the first three had hastened to marry, making bad choices and suffering the consequences. Kate, the youngest, smartest, and most attractive, had been guided by their mistakes, and had persisted with high school. Outstanding grades, SAT scores and teachers' recommendations had won her a full scholarship to U.S.C's school of architecture from where she hadn't looked back. She had met Peter in graduate school, recovered her faith in men, and proceeded to marry him. The rest was a fairy tale until today when two cataclysmic events had jolted her out of her idyllic existence.

"Perhaps the second is an antidote to the first," she thought, "who knows?"

Kate glanced at her watch. It was 11:30. They had been in the basement for almost an hour. Looking up, she noticed some of the people staring strangely at her.

"Can't blame them," she thought, "here I am sitting in a corner lost in my thoughts amidst all the chaos and uncertainty. I haven't spoken a word to them. They probably think a blunt heavy object fell on my head, or something."

Her thoughts were interrupted by a sudden, violent force pushing her backwards. Fortunately for her she had been sitting with her back against the basement wall. Her head, which had been leaning forward a bit, was thrown against the wall. She heard the thud of her head against the wall, a loud bang from somewhere upstairs and the panicked screams of people in the basement, all at once. Before she passed out, she caught a glimpse of arms, legs, bodies and a flurry of objects streaming towards her. She couldn't tell if the arms, legs and bodies were held together or not.

Kate regained consciousness about an hour later. As she opened her eyes, somebody who was fanning her shouted excitedly, "She's coming to, she's coming to!" A group of people gathered around her. It didn't look like anybody else had been hurt. Someone gave her something to drink and she gulped it down. That seemed to energize her. She stood up groggily and tottered about. The numbness in her head and legs began to recede. Within minutes, the manager in her had taken over and her body responded to her will. She could walk about freely now. She took a quick look. Everything seemed just like it had been.

"What happened?" She asked, nobody in particular.

"We don't know," a group of voices answered in unison.

It turned out that the rest of the people who had been sitting in groups in the middle of the basement had been spared any bodily damage, perhaps even death, by the neat row of mattresses and blankets which had been piled against the wall. They had cushioned their impact and had perhaps saved Kate's life as well. A whole pile of mattresses and blankets had covered Kate just before a swarm of bodies had landed on her.

"Incredible!" was all Kate could manage when she heard this account. The worst she had suffered in the face of what had seemed like all hell breaking loose, was a swelling on the back of her head which was still throbbing and aching, "Nothing a few Advils couldn't cure," she thought.

"Has anyone seen George?" She asked a few minutes later. Before anyone could answer, she realized George hadn't come down at all.

"George!" she shouted as she ran up the steps. The basement door was shut tight. Something heavy was blocking it. She called for help and several people came running up to lend a hand. It was no use. Some massive object had pinned the door down and there was nothing they could do about it. They decided it was probably the large conference table that had slid against the door. That must have been the loud bang. That's why George hadn't come down. He had been unable to move the table.

"How come he didn't knock on the door, or something?" someone asked.

"Maybe he did and no one heard him," someone else answered.

"This banging thing happened well after an hour after we came down. Why didn't he come down until then?" asked somebody.

No one had an answer. They left it at that feeling scared and uneasy and unwilling to probe other possibilities.

Kate decided to find the radio and turn it on to see if they had any updates. It had been over two hours since the emergency broadcast they had heard. "Stupid of me not to have thought of it earlier," she thought. She found the radio in a wooden cabinet attached to the wall. Luckily for them the cabinet had been latched. If not, the radio could have been damaged, and worse, hurt somebody as well. She twiddled the knobs until it came on. There was no sound. Just static. One of the people from her engineering staff strolled over and took a look.

"Hmm…," he said, "a brand new one. Damn good too. Extra sensitive enhanced reception for basement operation. I don't think it is getting any signals, except static."

They didn't like the sound of that. Why weren't any radio signals being transmitted?

"Maybe all the radio stations have broken down because of this earthquake activity," someone suggested.

"There are close to a 100 AM and FM stations in Southern California, don't tell me they've all broken down," someone voiced skepticism.

"And this radio must have at least a 200 mile range," said the engineer who had examined the radio.

"Let's call and find out what's going on," Kate said going over to the phone. She picked up the phone. There was no dialtone.

The gloomy silence that followed was broken by Kate's attempt at forced levity. "The rumbling seems to have spread to my stomach. Got to do something to stop it. Anyone else care to join me?" she asked pointing to the mini-pantry.

No one answered. They were not thinking of food. It was one of those eerie situations when everybody is thinking the same thing without a word having been said about what they are thinking. Kate's reference to rumbling had made them all realize that there was no sign of the earthquake. No rumbling, swaying or anything. They all broke into an involuntary shout of cheer. "Yeah!"

"Must have been the usual, short-lived tremor," said someone.

"It sure felt different, though," said someone else.

"Anyway, looks like it is all over now," said Kate.

"Except that the phone is dead and there are no radio signals," the engineer said darkly as if all the optimism was spoiling his fun. That made them all worry again. There was nothing they could do. The basement door was still shut tight. Suddenly they all felt very hungry and tired.

Kate decided against lighting the gas range. "Why run the risk of a gas leak?" she said.

Nobody protested. They were much too hungry and no one felt like cooking anyway. They made the most of the canned fruits, cheese, condensed milk and juices. Tasteless and spartan as it was, the lunch revived them.

A few minutes after lunch Kate said "Let me go see if we have any luck," and headed for the steps. This time when she tried the door it opened about three inches. Through the opening she could see one leg of the conference table. They had been right about the table blocking the basement door. In no time at all a couple of men had forced the door back another six inches and they streamed out of the basement, wary but elated.

Kate immediately went about looking for George. The main room had more of a look of devastation than before. Broken chairs, tables, lamps and other office supplies lay about everywhere. Kate could see no sign of structural damage. Not a window had shattered. "Perfect, flexible design," she muttered to herself, pleased that the building had suffered no damage. She went straight to George's office and almost stepped on his face.

George lay on the floor, across the doorway, at an angle. The lower half of his body pinned to the floor by the wardrobe which was wedged against the wall by the mahogany desk. Kate suppressed the scream in her throat. Mouth still open, she bent down to check his pulse. His pulse was fine. "Looks all right, probably just had a bad fall," she thought. The mahogany desk was too heavy for her and she had to get help. Soon they had George resting comfortably on the couch in the main room. He was breathing normally. It looked like he would regain consciousness soon. Kate got Diane, George's secretary, to watch George and then went about trying to assess the situation.

George needed medical attention. Neither the radio nor the phone was operational. Pretty much everybody, including Kate, was feeling jittery. Mothers worrying about kids, wives about husbands, boyfriends about girlfriends. She could feel the tension, though she no longer had anyone close enough to worry intensely about.

Some of the people had already gone out of the building to check things out. They came back and reported to Kate that it was much the same situation everywhere in the immediate neighborhood. Some injuries, a few serious. No phone. No radio. No further information.

Kate felt a mounting sense of frustration. Given the circumstances, it didn't look like anything really serious had happened. Then why the hell was there no radio, no phone, no sign of ambulances or fire trucks? In fact there was no sign of any relief activity. The streets were empty barring a few people walking about hesitantly. This was in stark contrast to the frenetic rescue activity she remembered in the aftermath of the 92 earthquake. Then, the mayor of LA had appeared on TV almost immediately to calm people down and to describe all the rescue efforts that were underway. Where was the Mayor now? Had anyone tried the TV? Maybe he was on TV. It was no use. When she turned on the wall-mounted TV in the main room, all she could see was the ghost images of the static.

Almost everybody was still in the main room, hanging around not knowing what to do. Too scared to venture out, too uneasy to settle down. Kate came to a quick decision. She turned to the people milling about.

"Guys," she said, "I'll drive around a bit and see if I can get any information. This won't do us any good, sitting around waiting for something to happen. I am not sure how safe the roads are. For all we know there could be electric shorts, gas leaks, fallen trees, collapsed roads.... who knows what else. I'll be back in about an hour or so. I don't want any of you to leave the building until I return."

They nodded meekly. She put Phil, the melancholy engineer, in charge and instructed him to get everyone into the basement, including George, if the rumblings resumed.

She didn't really have any fixed plan. She just started driving, got on to the nearest main road and headed east. She noticed nothing unusual. The roads looked good. There were no fallen trees or any rubble. She drove further east. She could see the Shearson Plaza building at a distance. It seemed OK. As she came nearer, though, she began to feel something was not right. The Shearson Plaza was a seven storied building. It was well known in that area because it was the only structure over two stories tall. It had been built before the township passed an ordinance limiting all buildings to two stories. It was a pretty old building, but had survived the 92 earthquake without so much as a scratch. The township had fought unsuccessfully to tear it down and had to give up when the courts ruled that any building that could survive the 92 earthquake could survive any foreseeable earthquake.

Kate couldn't tell for sure what was wrong. Shearson Plaza looked distinctly shorter. But it was in a wooded area so she didn't really have a clear view. "It could well be an optical illusion," she thought. After what she had been through, it wouldn't really have surprised her if she began to see two of everything. When she was about half a mile away from Shearson Plaza, Kate felt absolutely sure there was something wrong. Normally it rose well above the treeline at this point. But now it appeared to be barely 10 feet above the treeline. She got off the main road and headed towards Shearson Plaza. As she approached the building, she heard what sounded like screams coming from that direction. When she drove through the woods and came to the clearing, she was suddenly in full view of the disaster. Shearson Plaza had sunk three stories deep into the ground. All the upper floors seemed to be in tact. There did not appear to be any structural damage. It looked like the ground had simply caved in.

There were several people standing around. She could see a couple of police cars, fire trucks, and an ambulance. She stopped the car, got off, and walked towards the building. She found out from one of the lookers-on that the building had sunk around 11:30 in the morning. She correlated that immediately with the sudden force that had thrown her against the basement wall. The time seemed about right. Fortunately, most people had left the building at 10:30 when the emergency announcements came on. A few people had remained, some in the first three floors that were now buried. Those in the upper floors had taken the stairs and jumped out of the fourth floor windows which were just a few feet above the ground level. The rescue workers - a few policeman and firemen - had been able to pull out most of the people in the first three floors. But a part of the first floor had collapsed and two or three people were still trapped in there.

"It is as hot as hell in there. I don't know how long they will be able to hang on. Some people have gone looking for cranes and bulldozers to dig them up. I hope they make it in time," the man said.

Hot as hell in there. That was unlike any earthquake she had heard about. What George had said about a possibly unknown seismological phenomenon, came to her mind. She brushed the thought aside and went looking for a policeman. She had to find out if anybody knew what was happening. She found a policeman in one of the police cars.

"Any idea what's going on?" Kate asked him.

"Nope. A shame this," he said, pointing to the sunken building, "they should have torn it down."

"Why don't we have any news? Why aren't any relief operations underway? Do you realize people are going crazy with panic, not knowing what's happening and what to do?" she had raised her voice without realizing.

"Look lady, I am in the same boat myself. I don't even know if my wife and kids are safe. We are unable to reach head office in downtown LA. We made contact with a few local police stations. All we know is that quite a few tall buildings have gone down. Just like this one. Several hospitals."

"Where is the Mayor? Why isn't he on the air, addressing the people?"

"Can't reach the Mayor's office or the police headquarters. Don't know what good it would do even if we got them. There's no TV, no radio, no phone."

There wasn't much Kate could do there, so she got back to her car and continued east. She wanted to get to downtown LA and to the Mayor's office. Surely, they would have to have some information. At least now she knew that the local police didn't know much more than she did. This business about the tall buildings sinking into the ground with no structural damage whatsoever, really worried her. The possibility that this may not be an earthquake after all, was slowly dawning on her.

She got onto Santa Monica Freeway East and drove fast towards downtown LA. All along, the situation was the same. With no exception, all the tall buildings she could see had sunk. A few three and four storied buildings had sunk too, but not too many. None of the one and two storied buildings she saw had been affected. She didn't make any further stops to check things out. Her top priority now was to get to the Mayor's office.

Kate was somewhere near Century City when she saw a police car parked at a distance, lights flashing. There was a policeman next to it waving cars down. Quite a few cars had already lined up. Kate slowed down. When she came closer, she saw that the cars were not moving at all. They were at a stand still. None of the cars appeared to have any people inside. She turned the engine off, got off the car and started walking towards the policeman. She could now see that a sizable crowd had built up around the policeman. The road was at a steep upward incline, so she couldn't see what was holding up the traffic. As she walked toward the policeman, he caught sight of her, saw the quizzical expression on her face and simply pointed eastward in the direction of the road. Kate turned to follow the motion of his arm. Beyond where the policeman was standing, the road leveled and the visibility was uninterrupted as far as the eye could see. And Kate, for one, was not prepared for what her eyes saw. A quarter of a mile beyond where they stood the road disappeared into the steely blue of the Pacific.

Santa Monica Freeway had been ripped up for the second time in less than 6 years. The last time around they had fixed it in record time. It would be a while before they fixed it this time. Quite a while.

"Wwwwhaat...," Kate couldn't speak any further. The policeman simply nodded. For the first time, Kate noticed that the people around her looked petrified. Some were sobbing quietly. Most were too dumb struck to cry, or speak, or do anything. They simply stood there, not believing their eyes, losing faith in their senses, waiting to be told what to do.

CHAPTER 2

*G*eneral Paterson sat in his spacious office, hastily put back into working condition by his aides after the morning's tremors had wrought their havoc. He was a four star general and the highest ranking military officer in Southern California. Across from his desk sat Admiral Tyson, the chief of the Southern California Naval Command and General Garland, the chief of the Air Force base in Southern California. They all looked gloomy. They had good reason to be. Not only had they been through the uncertainties of the morning like anybody else, worse, now they knew what the situation was. It had taken them three hours to find out, but now they knew as much as anyone else in the world about what had happened, and more than anyone else in that part of the world with which they shared the most singular seismological manifestation in recorded history.

They had lost all communications capabilities that morning and that had upset them as much as, if not more than, the earthquake itself. They were just not used to it. It is common knowledge that the armed forces of the United States are paranoid about having access to secure communications, 24 hours a day, 365 days a year, under any conditions. Consequently, they had the most advanced, secure and reliable communications networks in the world. Not one, not two, many. The Army, Air Force, Navy, National Security Agency and the Department of Defense, each had its own separate communications network. Each network had at least double redundancy: a fully survivable fiber optic network and a backup satellite network. In addition, there was a federal communications network that tied all federal agencies together and in which the ranking officers of the armed forces enjoyed the highest priority. In spite of all this, the unthinkable had happened. They had lost contact with the rest of the world for approximately 2 hours and 30 minutes, starting at 11:30, at the moment of the big bang.

The land based fiber optic network was the first to go. Dead in a second as all the major feeder cables were severed. The satellite network collapsed less instantaneously as one satellite dish after another had been wrenched from the ground. They were somewhat unlucky not to have maintained radio contact. Ironically, they owed this to the compulsive obsession of the military with the latest gizmos. Had they continued with their simple, compact and powerful transceiver which could reach the continental U.S., Europe and Japan, they would most likely have been left with at least one channel of communication. But in just the past couple of months, in competition with one another, the Army, Air force and Navy had each replaced their old receiver with the latest steerable antenna technology which could be maneuvered to reach a single, isolated soldier anywhere in the world. And they had paid the price. Whereas the indoor transceiver would most likely have remained operational, the outdoor steerable antenna had met the same fate as the satellite dishes. Thus, it was, that each of the commanding officers had been left wringing his hands in helpless desperation like a common civilian.

The Army had been the first to get the satellite network going. The communications corps had been able to retrieve, repair and reinstall one of the satellite dishes. When General Paterson learnt, from the CNN special coverage, what had happened, his steely calm had deserted him and an unfamiliar panic had taken over. He had immediately sent messages to summon Admiral Tyson and General Garland. In the 30 minutes it took them to reach his office, several shots of whisky had worked their customary magic and General Paterson now looked his normal, composed, self. Externally at least.

"Gentlemen," he said, gesturing to General Garland and Admiral Tyson, "according to CNN, the portion of Southern California that we are on has been ripped off the mainland by a strong earthquake or some unknown seismological phenomenon. CNN reports that we are now approximately 100 miles from the mainland moving at a speed of about 5 miles per hour. The velocity at the moment of separation was apparently much higher. Around 80 miles per hour, or so. They don't have a handle yet on what caused this. At first they thought it was an earthquake. Now they don't think so. It is too early for a consensus expert opinion. All they know is that the break occurred parallel to the San Andrea's fault. Lot's of casualties, mostly on the mainland. Apparently, we are the lucky ones, though it is hard to believe that. Most of the rest of Southern California has been reduced to rubbles. Satellite pictures show lots of damage in our part as well. They have no idea why we are still afloat, or how much longer we will continue to be. CNN says that the separated landmass goes all the way from San Diego to Santa Barbara, parallel to the fault line. It is roughly 200 miles long and 20 miles wide. According to their estimates we have approximately 10 to 15 million people amongst us." He paused for breath. The other two were listening, mouth agape, face frozen in consternation.

"The Governor of California has requested federal assistance. President Walters has declared the entire

Southern California region a federal disaster area. I guess that still includes us." He had a wry smile on his face. "What beats me is why the media haven't swooped in on us. Maybe we were moving too fast for them. That couldn't be. Maybe they thought we just sank into the Pacific. That's it. That's probably what happened. They probably didn't realize we were still floating until the satellites tracked us down. In a couple of hours this place will be swarming with reporters. If we are still afloat and if they have the guts to land."

"You'll find at least one crazy son of a bitch looking for fame and fortune." Admiral Tyson had found his voice.

"This is one scary situation. I don't know how our troops and the civilians will react to it. Should we make this information public or not?" General Garland asked.

"They are bound to know sooner or later. There are plenty of Cable TV companies in these parts. Once they fix their satellite dishes and the broken cables, everyone will come to know. If that happens, we will have mass hysteria on our hands. By now, some people must have already discovered that we have separated from the mainland. They won't know the details. But they will be aware of the painful fact that we are floating somewhere in the middle of the Pacific. Fortunately, all communications networks are down. So there is no way the news can spread, except by word of mouth. We have maybe until tomorrow before it becomes common knowledge. We have to release the information in a controlled and orderly fashion, so people don't panic. We've got to do it within the next few hours. Most of the civilian areas have probably lost power, so it will be too dangerous to move about after dark. I would like to contact my commanding

23

officer for instructions, would you gentlemen please wait over there," General Paterson pointed to the adjoining room, "It has a TV. You can get updates." He didn't want them in his presence when he talked to his superior. He had tried to reach the Army Chief of Staff earlier but hadn't succeeded. The Army headquarters in Washington D.C. had not been very helpful; they were getting their news from CNN too.

General Paterson did not like dealing with civilian matters. Having spent over 30 years in military bases, he had almost forgotten what civilian life was like. He had gotten used to the black and white life of a military man where one either took orders and executed them or gave orders to be executed. The shades of gray in which civilian life was steeped, discomfited him. But he had no choice. Like it or not, he was the highest ranking person with full knowledge of the situation, and he had to act on it. He dialed the Army Chief's number. Someone answered before he even heard a single ring.

"General Paterson, is that you? Took your bloody time, didn't you?"

"Sir, yes sir. I mean no sir. All networks were down. Called as soon as I could," He was standing in attention, without quite realizing.

"What's the situation there?"

"Not sure sir. All we know is what we heard from CNN. Doesn't look good."

"A bloody fine mess isn't it. What do you plan to do about it?" The voice was more sympathetic now.

"Precisely why I called, sir. I need instructions. We are the only ones who know. We need to figure out a way to break the news to the public. Request permission to deploy our troops for the purpose sir."

"Permission granted. Do whatever it takes. But first make sure the Army base is safe. Call me if you have updates. I'll let the Defense Secretary and the Chairman of the Joint Chiefs of Staff know. Good bye and good luck."

Years of experience in planning military strategy came in handy. Within half an hour, the three of them had worked out a plan. The people, both military and civilian, would be given partial information; they probably couldn't handle all of it at once. They would release information in a controlled manner. No lies, but not the whole truth either. Each of them would first personally address the troops under their command and inform them of the situation. They would pool their resources and send out messengers to every police station. Each police chief would be personally briefed of the situation. The police chiefs would then be asked to send police officers door-to-door to inform all the residents. The message to be conveyed was the following: at 11:30 a.m. the part of Southern California they were in had experienced a major earthquake cutting off TV, phone and electricity. They had been pushed into the ocean and separated from the rest of Southern California, but the situation was expected to be temporary. The President had authorized emergency relief measures and evacuation would be underway within a day or so. Phone, radio, TV and power would be restored soon. There was plenty of food and water, so there was no shortage. Everyone was requested to stay off the roads, be calm and cooperate.

They also decided that while the message was being conveyed they would dispatch all communications engineers and technicians who could be spared to assess the damage to the phone and cable TV networks and to start fixing them. They created a joint scout patrol consisting of a thousand troops to cover as much of the land area as they could before nightfall, to assess the damage. They decided to meet again at 9:00 p.m. in General Paterson's office, after the reports from the scout patrol came in, to figure out the next steps.

Shortly before Kate returned to her office worrying about how best to break the news to her colleagues, how much to tell them, and so on, a policeman had told them everything. All the expected reactions had occurred, and partial calm had been restored by the time Kate got back. Kate was surprised that they already knew. She told them what she had seen and they told her what they had heard. After much crying and consoling, they decided to go home to check on their families. Fortunately, they all lived within a 5 mile radius, so no one found themselves 100 miles away from home. Kate asked them not to return to work until they heard from her.

Kate dropped George off at his house. He still felt dizzy and wasn't quite up to driving, but otherwise seemed all right. Kate was glad his wife was home. She comforted George's wife, promised to call the next day and headed home. On the way home, Kate realized that Peter wouldn't be coming home that night. His office was in downtown LA. She wouldn't be seeing him or hearing from him for a while. "I hope the poor slob is all right," she said to herself, surprised that she still cared for him. "Probably shacked up with his Chinese friend in some downtown hotel," she thought, "maybe even reading Shakespeare. Good time to read Tempest, the mood and the ambience would be right." Suddenly she felt lonely and desolate. She started crying. All the bottled up feelings burst out in hard, violent sobs. By the time she reached home, she had stopped crying and was feeling a lot better.

CHAPTER 3

*I*t was around 5:30 p.m. when Kate got home. She made herself some coffee and sat down to drink. Soon she found the same old thoughts racing through her head. First Peter, then the tremors, and then the horrifying picture of Santa Monica freeway disappearing into the ocean. The normally warm and pleasant little house seemed dark and morbid. The cheerless silence in the house resonated with the negative thoughts in her head and they fed each other until she could no longer bear it. The uncertainty of the situation bothered her too. Not knowing where they were, what had happened, how long they would remain afloat - a thousand questions and no answers. She decided she had to keep herself busy, and the best thing to do would be to find out more about this phenomenon. It was unlikely that their office would open any time soon, and she had to keep herself occupied. "Let me see, where do I start? No phone, no radio, no TV. How am I going to find out more?" she thought. After agonizing over this for a while, it occurred to her that the only avenue of pursuit left to her was the sole source of concrete information she had, had, the whole day. She had to go find the policeman who had come to their office and probe him for more information.

She drove to the Marina Del Rey police station. Only the policechiefwasin,theotherswerestilloutontheirdoor-to-door beat. She was unsure what to do. She had never been in a police station before, much less talked to a police chief. The police chief was absorbed in writing something and didn't notice her. She was still debating whether she should try the damsel in distress approach, or the outraged citizen approach, or the dumb and innocent approach, when, with a rustle of papers, the chief looked up, saw her, and said, "Can I help you, Ma'am?"

"Yes, please," she found herself saying, "you see, my husband hasn't come home yet, and I'm worried. His office is in downtown LA. I don't know if he is stuck somewhere. I am all so confused with this earthquake thing. Could you please tell me if you have any more information?"

The Chief felt sorry for her. "I sure wish I could help you. All I know is what the military folks told me and you've probably heard that from one of my men," he said.

"Military folks? What military folks?" Kate asked sharply.

"Well, an army sergeant brought the news to me in the afternoon, said he was acting on General Paterson's orders."

"Who's General Paterson?"

"He is the chief of the Army base in Mission Viejo."

"How did he find out?"

"I don't know," it had never occurred to him to ask.

Kate didn't waste any more time with him after that. She got directions from the Chief to get to the Army base, and set off. When she arrived at the base, it was a quarter to nine. The guard at the gate stopped her car.

"I am here to see General Paterson," Kate told him.

"Do you have an appointment?" he asked.

"No.."

The guard wouldn't let her finish. "I'm sorry, you can't get in without permission," he snapped.

"Look here," Kate said suddenly inspired, "I am from the Mayor's office and I've got to see General Paterson. How do you suppose I can make an appointment with the phones down? It's an emergency and I must see him."

The guard was confused. If someone from the Mayor's office wanted to see the General, it was probably important. On the other hand he couldn't let a civilian in without approval. "Do you have an ID?" he asked.

Kate pretended to leaf through her purse. "Must have left it behind," she said apologetically.

The guard thought for a minute. "Miss, why don't you wait here while I send for permission," he said. Kate nodded. He called a private and gave him instructions.

Clearly, General Paterson was anxious to make contact with the Mayor's office, for a few minutes later the General's aide personally drove down and escorted her to the conference room where General Paterson was waiting for his 9:00 p.m. meeting with Admiral Tyson and General Garland. When Kate entered, General Paterson rose to meet her.

"Kate Upshaw, Mayor Taylor's press secretary," Kate introduced herself, quite calmly. She was all nervous and knotted up inside. Would they court-martial her or something of that sort, she wondered. It was too late now, she had to go on with the charade.

"Glad to meet you," the General shook hands warmly. "What word from the Mayor?"

"I don't know. I didn't go into work today, I wasn't feeling well. I was hoping I could get some information from you about how I can get in touch with the Mayor," she said, surprised at the smooth stream of lies pouring out of her. Maybe she should be the Mayor's press secretary, she thought, she seemed well qualified.

"Oh, shit!" General Paterson couldn't conceal his frustration. "I was expecting the Mayor to assume control of the civilian affairs."

In the confusion of the day's events, the General had missed the CNN report about how both the Mayor and the Deputy Mayor of LA were out in Washington for a meeting of the nation's mayors.

Kate was in an opportunistic frame of mind. "Yes, General," she said without hesitation, "he will. Or rather, I will, on his behalf, until we get in touch with him."

This press secretary thing was growing on her. From a scrupulously honest person to a maven of manipulation, the transformation had only taken minutes. Perhaps it was a subconscious urge to escape her personal situation. Perhaps she was simply rising to the occasion to meet the challenge. She didn't know. She would sort that out later. She was spared any further questioning by the arrival of Admiral Tyson and General Garland.

Kate must have been pretty convincing, for General Paterson introduced her as Mayor Taylor's press secretary. Both Admiral Tyson and General Garland appeared relieved to hear who she was. They shared General Paterson's dislike of all things civilian and were only too willing to hand over the responsibility of civilian operations. Kate had come up with a great stratagem, quite unwittingly. She was just what the three military men needed. An official excuse to unburden themselves of the undesirable civilian chores that had been thrust upon them.

General Paterson opened the meeting on a positive note. He had been feeling pretty good ever since President Walters had contacted him earlier in the afternoon. That had virtually assured him the five star rank he had been coveting for a long time. He told them how the President approved of the steps they were taking and the assurances he had given. It made them feel good to know that the President was personally involved and had made their safety his top priority.

Next came the report from the Scout Patrol. They had organized the Scout Patrol into three units. One unit had been asked to report on the southern sector, one was assigned to the northern sector and the third to the central sector which included the vicinity of the base. An officer had been placed in charge of each unit. The three unit leaders were now waiting to report their findings.

All three of them had pretty much the same story to tell. There was no phone, radio, TV or power anywhere. Tall buildings had sunk several stories deep. No structural damage anywhere. Roads were fine. Casualties numbered over a thousand. Lots of injuries, mostly broken arms, legs and the like. Some were serious. The breakaway landmass extended a little beyond San Diego, almost to the Mexican border, to the south, way past Ventura almost up to Santa Barbara in the north, and right through the heart of LA to the east. The most eerie aspect of their findings was this: in all directions, ground temperature close to the ocean was very high, about 150 degrees Fahrenheit on the eastern side and around 175 degrees Fahrenheit on the west. So much so, most of the people living within a distance of about 2000 feet from the ocean had fled their homes and taken shelter inland, in churches, schools, public buildings, whatever they could find. This had fascinated and frightened Kate and reminded her of what the man at Shearson Plaza had told her about the sunken first floor being very hot.

The second piece of news to surprise and scare Kate was the report about the LA Airport. The two Generals and the Admiral had not been as concerned as they had already witnessed similar incidents in their own bases. All the heavy aircraft that had been on the ground at the time of the big bang, around 11:30 a.m., had sunk deep into the ground. Most helicopters and small two seaters were unharmed. They had seen the same thing at the military bases. Heavy transport aircraft like the B1 had sunk while the lighter fighter planes like the F16s and F18s were fine.

"Something to do with the ground pressure distribution," thought Kate, "it sounds like there is a critical pressure threshold beyond which the ground just caves in." But she didn't say a word. She was, after all, the press secretary and couldn't possibly be aware of such technical matters. She was worried, really worried. But she kept her thoughts to herself.

All boats and ships that were docked at the time of breaking away had been irreparably damaged by the impact. Most had sunk. Several cruise liners had sunk and hundreds of people had perished. Again, this was not news to the military chiefs as the Navy vessels docked at the naval base had met a similar fate. But Kate was aghast.

This was one gigantic, unmitigated disaster that kept getting worse, the more information she got. The only good news was that people generally appeared calm. There was no mass hysteria, frenzy, or any unruly behavior. "Perhaps too dazed and confused," Kate thought, "let's see how they behave tomorrow when they learn more about their plight."

When all the reports had been made, General Paterson let out a weary sigh and exclaimed, "We are trained to fight, but not against nature."

General Garland and Admiral Tyson nodded agreement. Something spurred Kate to remark, "General, but we are not fighting nature, we are just trying to survive. We can, and must, do that." All three were taken aback at that.

General Paterson asked Kate to be back the next morning at 8:00 a.m. to attend another meeting with him, General Garland and Admiral Tyson. "We will assess the situation in light of the latest information available and allocate responsibilities. We'd really rather have somebody else take responsibility for the civilian side of it," he said. Kate assured the General that she was ready to step up and substitute for the Mayor until he could be contacted. She was issued a special pass that let her enter all three bases at any time of the day or night. She was now in the thick of it.

CHAPTER 4

*T*he first TV reporter landed on the breakaway landmass at about 10:00 p.m. He was from KBEE, the "We Keep You Abuzz," channel, a local LA station that was the most popular one in Southern California. His name was Randy Freeman. He was young, ambitious, and smart. He had fought with his station manager for three hours, threatened to quit, lured him with the incredible pictures and breaking stories he would come back with. But the station manager had been firm.

"Too risky to do it until they give us some more information," he had said, "we are not even sure where it is."

A quick call to a contact in NASA had settled that, he had obtained the exact latitude and longitude of the floating landmass and a promise to keep him updated every half hour. The station manager had still refused. What finally clinched the deal was a flash of inspiration on Randy's part. He had suggested that the main focus could be the reaction from the Hollywood celebrities.

"Picture interviews with Tom Cruise, Harrison Ford, Sandra Bullock, Julia Roberts,....Steven Spielberg, James Camerone,....My God! James Camerone! I would ask him 'Mr. Camerone, you raised the Titanic to a new height, what would you do if this were an action thriller, where do you see this floating disaster going?' Imagine how the public would react to his views. We've got to do this. Think of what the Desert Storm did to CNN. We are already number one in Southern California, we'll easily be number one in the entire United States. We can write our own tickets after that."

The temptation had been too much, the manager had given in. Neither of them had paused to think what frame of mind the superstars would be in, or for that matter whether it was appropriate to air celebrity reactions when people didn't even know if their loved ones were alive or whether they would see them again, alive or dead. Randy may have, but he wasn't going to share such thoughts with his manager.

"OK, but a small crew. A helicopter, a pilot, a cameraman and you. That's it. We've got to keep this very discreet. We are probably going to be in violation of INS rules, coast guard rules,.. who knows what else," the station manager had said.

"Don't worry, we are still going to be within the U.S. boundaries. It is just that the boundary is fast moving." Randy had jokingly assured him that he would take all possible precautions.

"Sneak out and sneak back in the dark. No one will notice in the middle of this confusion."

Randy had hoped to reach Hollywood by 8:30 p.m. so he could take some pictures while there was still some daylight left. But it had been harder to locate the landmass than he had anticipated. The last update he had from his NASA contact had been around 7:30 p.m. He was now out of range to keep radio contact with his LA office going.

He hadn't expected that it would be so difficult to spot a two hundred mile stretch of land. But then, a two hundred mile stretch of land in the vast nothingness of the Pacific is just a spec. In fact, he had been very lucky to sight it around 9:30 p.m., after circling around for almost an hour. The pilot had been telling him for a while that they had to abandon and return, or they would be dangerously low on fuel. But Randy was running on a different kind of fuel. His greed was his fuel and his ego his engine. He had a large engine and an unlimited supply of fuel. He had coaxed the pilot to keep looking for a few more minutes. Finally, when even Randy was ready to give up, the cameraman had spotted it. Some scattered lights a few miles away had led them to the floating landmass.

Once they sighted land, locating Hollywood had not been a problem. Even in the dark, the pilot had been able to find his way in that familiar terrain. It had been frustrating for the cameraman, for he hadn't been able to take many pictures. An occasional shot here and a shot there when the searchlight from the helicopter caught something interesting. Randy had instructed the pilot to fly straight to Beverly Hills. They would worry about the other pictures later, he had thought. They could even blend some of the aerial shots that had been coming in via satellite, with his celebrity interviews. The important thing was to get the celebrity interviews, they could improvise on the background material later.

When the helicopter approached Beverly Hills, it was dark and deathly still. A few of the mansions had their own generators, but the others were dark except for the flickering candles. He hadn't expected Spielberg and company to be standing in the street corner waving to him, but this was disappointing. He asked the pilot to touch down right in the middle of Sunset Boulevard. As he got off the helicopter, he noticed movement behind the high fences that surrounded most of the mansions.

The first person he talked to was a businessman. He had come out to check if it was the rescue mission President Walters had promised. He was disappointed that it was not, but Randy convinced him that his views would be important to persuade people back home that it was worth mounting a large rescue operation, no matter what the cost.

"It will keep the pressure on the politicians," he had said.

After that the businessman had railed and ranted about the inconveniences he had suffered, the loss to his business, and so forth. Randy got a few good shots of him and his family. By then the camera lights had attracted more people. They were scattered about on the sidewalk, standing at a distance, watching curiously.

Randy scanned the people anxiously. Not a single celebrity face. Forget superstars, not even a face he could recognize, and he knew all of them down to the most insignificant starlet. He walked up and down Sunset Boulevard, the cameraman in tow. An obese, middle-aged man sidled up to him. He thrust a thick wad of money into Randy's hands.

"All hundred dollar bills," he said, "that's a hundred thousand. There will be more later. A million. All you have to do is take my wife and me back. Just the two of us, we have no kids."

Randy was stunned. He hadn't anticipated this, but it made perfect sense. He would have given anything to get the hell away from this floating wreck too. And money meant nothing to these people.

"Sorry, can't do it," he said, "the helicopter can only take three people. We have no room."

The man raised his offer to ten million, in cash, right there, if Randy and the cameraman would stay back while the pilot dropped him and his wife off. The pilot could return in a few hours to get them. This was serious money. More than he would see even if KBEE made it to number one in the country. But it was too risky. The station manager would find out. And then he would lose the money, his job, perhaps even go to jail. The idea was something to think about, though. Maybe he would go back and strike a deal with someone to airlift the mega-rich at ten million a pop. There had to be private companies that would take him up on this. He would look into it.

He brushed the man off and headed back to the helicopter. He had a few interviews recorded. Nothing sensational. At least they were all zillionaires, and that always attracted attention. He had a few good shots of women crying, hugging their babies and begging to know what was going on. He had interviewed a six year old boy and his eight year old sister who were alone at home with their nanny; their parents were away in Europe. The kids had been terrified. They knew something was very wrong, but could not comprehend what had happened. That would make a great story. Not what he had come here for, but something to go on.

They got back in the helicopter. The pilot was getting ready to lift off. The people still hovered around the sidewalk, staring at them. Randy was thinking about whether the station manager would be mad at him. He had failed at what he set out to do. Perhaps he had just enough to justify the trip. Just then, an idea occurred to him. He asked the pilot to turn the engine off and told the cameraman to go down with his gear and record the crowd's reaction. When the cameraman asked Randy what reaction he expected, he answered, "I am going to announce over the PA system that we can take one family back with us. Just one. Whoever reaches the helicopter first will make it."

"Are you crazy? You know we can't do that. We have no room. Even if we did, it would be against the rules," the cameraman said.

"I know, I know. I have no intentions of taking anybody. I just want some good shots of these rich bastards trying to beat the hell out of each other to save their own butts. It'll make a great story, partially compensate for the celebrity interviews we don't have."

The cameraman stared at him incredulously, "It is not right, Randy," he said, "you can't play with people's emotions like that. Especially people in their state of mind."

"Just do it please!" Randy snapped. "It will do no harm and make our jobs easier. Who will ever find out? We will probably report it as the frenzied reaction of the superrich of Beverly Hills trying to take over the helicopter to save their own lives."

The cameraman got off with his gear reluctantly and walked away from the helicopter.

"Take good shots of people rushing toward the helicopter," Randy shouted after him. "Make sure no one runs you over. They'll probably rush in from both sides."

The cameraman walked to a point about 150 feet away from the front of the helicopter and positioned himself, his video camera ready, facing the helicopter.

Randy picked the microphone up and announced, "Folks, I have just been in touch with my LA office. They've authorized me to bring back one family. No more than five people, that's all we have room for. Whoever makes it to the helicopter first can take their family with them."

Even Randy had not anticipated the reaction that followed. It was a mad melee as the people rushed toward the helicopter from all sides. The nearest people were about 400 feet away. It was quite a sight, in the posh surroundings of Beverly Hills, to watch a swarm of people, young and old, men, women and children, run like they were possessed, toward the helicopter. Some children fell and were trampled upon. People were screaming hysterically. They ran, eyes blinded by sweat and tears, uncaring, heedless of the others, each intent on getting there first to ensure their family's safety.

Watching this from his vantage point, Randy started to feel scared. What would this mob do to them when they discovered the truth, he wondered. Probably beat them to death. They had to get away before the crowd got to them. He turned to the pilot and said, "Let's go, take off!"
"But,..." the pilot hesitated.

"Hurry, hurry, let's take off," he urged the pilot.

"What about him?" the pilot asked pointing to the cameraman.

"We'll come back for him later. Leave, leave!" Randy shouted.

"We don't have enough fuel left to circle around and return. Also, we can't just leave him there, the mob may beat the hell out of him."

"Just take off, damn you!"

The pilot had hesitated a little too long. Even before he could turn the engine back on and engage the rotor, the mob was upon them, screaming like hyenas. As the crowd converged on them, the ground started rocking. There was a loud noise and the ground caved in right under the helicopter, taking down the helicopter and the mass of people surrounding it. Where the helicopter stood minutes ago, there was a gaping hole roughly 40 feet in diameter. Most of the people died, crushed by the helicopter, before it burst into flames. After that, the rest of them died a slow and agonizing death. The crowd above could hear them screaming for quite some time. The cameraman got great shots of all this. His hands shivering, mind in a panic, he continued to record without thinking.

Kate had been right, pressure distribution on the ground was critical. At the moment of breaking away, the depth of the earth's crust in the separated landmass had been critically influenced by the prevailing ground pressure distribution. Any significant change to the pressure distribution could not be supported by the ground. They would find out more about all this later.

CHAPTER 5

P resident Walters had been alerted when the first tremors had hit Southern California around ten-thirty in the morning. He had been told that it was just the run of the mill seismic activity so common in that area. The president had asked the White House Chief of Staff to monitor the situation closely and let him know how it developed. When the situation did develop in an extraordinary and unprecedented manner around 11:30, no one had been prepared for it. The Chief of Staff had pulled the President out of his scheduled meeting with some visiting foreign dignitaries and had set up an emergency meeting with the Secretary of Defense and the Secretary of State.

The President and his two senior cabinet members had been briefed. The first reports had been sketchy. They had been told that a massive earthquake had torn Southern California apart and that a sizable portion of it had disappeared into the Pacific, presumed sunk. Like everyone else, they too had reacted with horror and disbelief. They had then watched the first coverage of the disaster on CNN, had seen for themselves the magnitude of the destruction and the reigning chaos, and reality had registered.

At first sabotage had been suspected. But intelligence reports had soon negated this. There simply were no known explosives that could cause damage on this scale. Nuclear bombs could do it, but there was no nuclear cloud, radioactive fallout, or massive fires characteristic of a nuclear explosion. A nuclear explosion of that magnitude

43

would have reduced the entire Southern California region including the breakaway landmass, to a rubble with very few survivors. It had to be seismic activity of some sort, some kind of a hitherto unknown combination of an earthquake and a volcano, was the opinion that had emerged.

President Walters had stubbornly refused to believe that a two hundred-mile stretch of land could disappear into the Pacific without a trace. He had immediately ordered NASA and CIA to reposition all satellites they possibly could, to scour that part of the Pacific. Hundreds of military planes from Air Force bases in the rest of California, Arizona and Nevada had been asked to fly over the Pacific in search patterns. Some of them had been equipped with the most advanced acoustic and infrared sensing devices on earth. The first breakthrough had come from a NASA remote sensing satellite, which had picked up radio signals coming from the Pacific about one hundred miles from the Southern California coast. This information had been passed on to the CIA who had confirmed shortly after, that, that was indeed the breakaway landmass.

President Walters had wept openly when he saw the first pictures of scattered, dazed, people walking around on nearly deserted roads. The sight of ordinary citizens moving about in what appeared to be their usual, placid, surroundings, unaware of the extent of the tragedy that had befallen them, had touched something deep within him that even he was unaware existed. He had immediately made up his mind that his top priority would be the safe evacuation of the approximately 10 million people on the floating landmass. The disaster area in the mainland would be second priority. Not that that was less important, at least they understood the situation there. He had been in touch with the Governor of California and had promised him all necessary federal assistance. Relief operations were well underway. They knew how to deal with it.

The floating landmass was quite another story. They did not have the foggiest idea of the situation there. They had seen the pictures. They had a good idea of the surface damage. What was missing was an understanding of what was happening beneath the surface. They simply had no idea what had caused the separation or what was keeping that multi-trillion ton landmass afloat.

President Walters' first reaction had been to deploy all available transport planes and start evacuating the area immediately. His defense secretary had informed him that they probably had about 500 transport planes within the continental U.S. and Hawaii, ready for deployment. Another 2000 could be obtained within eight to ten hours from various U.S. air force bases in the Atlantic and the Pacific and from their NATO allies and Japan. That was a total of 2500 transport planes at their disposal. Assuming each could carry 300 people at a time on average and could complete the round-rip from California to the floating landmass in about three hours, that would have meant 750000 people evacuated every three hours. 6,000,000 people in a day, assuming round-the-clock operation. It would still take one to two days to get all the ten to twelve million people out. There was no assurance that the floating landmass would still be floating until then. President Walters' eyes had welled up again with visions of millions of people waving goodbye from the sinking landmass, as the last transport plane departed. It was hopeless, but the best plan they could think of.

Their theoretical deliberations had been ended abruptly by a fresh set of pictures from the CIA satellites. It had

45

shown heavy aircraft, both civilian and military, buried deep in the ground all over the floating landmass. Not a single large airplane that was fit to fly could be seen. Just helicopters and light aircraft. They were useless for an evacuation of this scale. The conclusion had been obvious. The landmass, for whatever reason, could not support the weight of the heavy aircraft.

That had led to a new plan. If evacuation by air was infeasible, then why not evacuation by sea? Quick calculations had followed. Assumptions had been made about how many ships, military and civilian, including aircraft carriers and cruise liners, could be obtained. It had turned out that if all of the world's largest ships could be assembled, then the entire evacuation could be completed in two to four days. Reasonable, but the catch was that it would take weeks, if not months, to get the ships from Europe, Asia, Africa and Australia. Again the same crucial question: would the landmass be still floating? Added to that was a new dimension. The landmass had been moving at about 5 miles per hour. That meant it would have drifted about 3500 miles from the California coast by then. The effect of the drifting could be partially alleviated by coordinating the routes taken by ships from different countries and managing it so that they would intercept the floating landmass at different points along its trajectory. It would be a logistical nightmare, but it could be done. This evacuation plan would require global coordination. They decided that this was the best avenue of pursuit.

President Walters entrusted Admiral Roland, the Navy Chief of Staff, with the task of coordinating the evacuation. By a special presidential decree, every single ship on the western coast, military or civilian, U.S. or foreign, was commandeered. That gave them a total of 225 to start with.

The fastest of them could reach the floating landmass in approximately 15 hours. If only the landmass could remain floating, there was hope. They decided it was best not to make the evacuation plan public as there were still far too many uncertainties and details to be ironed out. The last thing they needed was some distortion by the news media, which could launch a public outcry.

All available cabinet members and the senior White House staff were entrusted with the task of contacting all friendly countries known to have large ships and persuade them to turn over control of these ships, including their crew, to Admiral Roland to facilitate evacuation coordination. By 3:00 p.m. the first ships had already left the bases in central and northern California to intercept the floating landmass. The fastest of them would reach the destination around 6:00 a.m. the next morning.

While in the midst of developing an evacuation plan, President Walters had received word that General Paterson had made contact and had learned of the steps the General had initiated. The President had been ecstatic. He had immediately called General Paterson to congratulate him on the measures he had taken and to assure him his fullest possible support. He had asked the General to bypass his normal chain of command and report directly to him. General Paterson had also been given the President's private phone number and told that he could call the President at any time of the day or night.

President Walters had by now addressed all angles but one. They had to get a fundamental understanding of the phenomenon that caused the separation. This knowledge was vital in determining how long the landmass would continue to float, and, consequently, was central to the entire evacuation plan. He wanted the best scientific experts on the subject assembled at the White House by that evening. He planned to personally address them to explain the gravity of the situation and to motivate them to put their collective brainpower to work, to unravel the baffling mystery. He instructed his staff to track down the presidents of MIT, Harvard, Caltech, Princeton, University of California Berkeley, and Stanford, and then personally got on the phone with each one of them to explain the situation and ask them to volunteer their best experts in Seismology, Geology and Geophysics. Other experts could be added as needed later. He had already appointed Lieutenant Strand, the technical advisor to the Air force Chief of Staff, and generally acknowledged to be the best scientific mind in the entire military, as the chairman of the Special Council on the Separation Phenomenon. It now remained to be seen what the council would unearth. Quite literally.

CHAPTER 6

*A*dmiral Roland had gone about his job meticulously. Within hours of being asked by the President to lead the sea evacuation effort, he had contacted each and every captain in charge of the 225 ships available for deployment on the west coast. He had sworn them to secrecy and then proceeded to describe the evacuation plan. They had all been quite supportive and listened with enthusiasm. Even the captains of cruise liners who had the unenviable task of getting thousands of passengers off board without really being able to give a convincing explanation, had participated willingly. The magnitude of the disaster and the plight of the people on the breakaway landmass had touched everyone's heart.

In quick time, they had together determined the best sea-route to intercept the floating landmass. They had planned everything. Food, first aid, nurses and doctors called in from various military bases and hospitals, everything. Admiral Roland had briefed them on the condition of the floating landmass. The CIA pictures showing the sunken buildings and aircraft had been sent to every captain. They had decided that since the landmass was moving at about 5 m.p.h., it would be very tricky for the ships to dock. Not only would they have to coordinate the ships' speed to maintain zero velocity relative to the floating landmass, they would have to find suitable points along the coast for docking.

Practically all of the harbors on the Southern California coastline had suffered serious damage. The best alternative had appeared to be to approach within about a couple of thousand feet of the landmass and then send in small motor powered life boats ashore to ferry the people. This would take considerably longer to fill up each ship, but they had thought it would be a lot safer and justified the extra delay.

Admiral Roland had asked the fastest of the ships, a frigate from the naval base in Monterey, to lead the landing effort. They were to first send in a surveillance party to determine the best landing approach for the small boats, and then contact General Paterson to brief him of the evacuation plan. Admiral Roland would then discuss with General Paterson the details of the evacuation. They would need General Paterson's help to determine how many landing points there should be along the coast. They had assumed it would be far too dangerous to attempt to land on the eastern side as the landmass was likely to be more unstable there. They would need General Paterson to verify that. If, with some luck, their assumptions turned out to be invalid and the landmass could support evacuation from the eastern side as well, that would be so much better. They could then pick evacuation points all around the landmass and then coordinate a smooth and orderly evacuation. General Paterson's role in this would, of course, be critical. He would have to arrange for people to be transported to the evacuation points in small groups without creating panic. If the general public came to know and stormed the evacuation points, that would be an unmitigated disaster. They could trust General Paterson to handle all this.

Admiral Roland, a cautious and conservative man by nature, had decided not to inform General Paterson of the evacuation plan ahead of time. It was not that he distrusted General Paterson. He was not sure how secure the communications line was with all that had transpired. If there was a leak and people on the floating landmass got wind of it, the entire plan could be endangered. Therefore, with much reluctance, he had refrained from intimating General Paterson of the evacuation plan. He knew this would entail significant delays in starting the evacuation procedure, but that could not be helped. As a result, the role of the frigate from Monterey was much more significant than all the other ships. The frigate had two key jobs: to determine the landing approach and to contact General Paterson and brief him. Admiral Roland had drilled this repeatedly into the captain of the frigate.

It was now getting to be 5:00 a.m. and the frigate was within half a mile of the landmass. It was still semi-dark; sunrise wouldn't be for another half hour. The captain of the frigate stood on the deck gazing at the landmass in astonishment. He had still not quite come to grips with the reality of seeing the Southern California coastline some 300 miles inside the Pacific. It looked so beautiful and placid, as it always did. He had seen it a thousand times before and it looked no different now. Its motion was barely perceptible; it needed a trained eye to discern it. His heart swelled with pride at the thought of the role he was playing in determining the fate of the people stuck over there.

They had had no trouble at all locating it. The closest ship behind them was at least two hours away. That would give them plenty of time to determine the best landing approach, contact General Paterson to brief him, and then report to Admiral Roland. All they would have to do then was to go to the appropriate landing point as instructed by Admiral Roland or General Paterson, fill up the ship with as many of the evacuees as possible, probably around 200, and then head back. He would be doing this many times in the next few weeks, he thought. If the landmass continued to float... who knew what could happen.

The captain took the frigate to within 2000 feet of the coastline and gave instructions to maintain position. He had already picked three of his best men for the surveillance party. The captain had given them clear instructions.

"Be extremely careful," he had told them, "in all probability this is going to be a routine landing. But we've never done this kind of thing before. The shore maybe different, unstable, whatever... I don't know. They know nothing about what's causing all this, so we have to be very cautious. Remember, you guys are the guinea-pigs being sent out there to find out what it's like. You are clearing the way for the rest of us. After the first landing, the others will be a piece of cake."

They had laughed at him and made fun of him for being melodramatic. "Don't worry captain," one of them had said, "we are prepared. For everything. Even for the Pacific cousin of the Lochness monster." They didn't know it, but they were not.

They lowered the boat with the surveillance party into the water and watched them move away. The captain had his binoculars trained on them. They were now about 500 feet from the shore. Everything looked fine. They would be ashore in less than half a minute. They were about 50 feet away when the captain noticed there was something wrong. The boat appeared to be wobbling, out of control. Before he could say anything his radio came alive.

"Captain, we're in trouble," he could hear one of his men, the same man who had so insouciantly remarked that he was ready to fight sea monsters, saying, "something hot's burning through the boat. We're going to turn back, I don't think we can approach from this side."

That's the last the captain heard from them. They had no chance to turn back. Within seconds the molten rock pouring out of the landmass had seared through the boat. The boat had virtually no bottom left. As the captain watched in horror, the three men jumped into the water and the molten rock burnt through their skin. They didn't even attempt to swim. They just bobbed up and down a few times, arms flailing about, screaming in pain. Then they went down. Death was quick, though agonizing. They were engulfed by the molten rock which solidified on contact with the body. All three were dead before they hit the bottom.

This was a tragedy that could have been averted had they waited for another day for the first reports from the special council on the separation phenomenon. The scientists would have known that the phenomenon had to involve some kind of volcanic activity spewing hot gases and molten rock into the ocean. It was too late for the three men.

Tears streaming down his face, the captain of the frigate got on the phone with Admiral Roland. The first approach had failed, he explained. He had lost three men and a boat. He didn't know the reason, but there appeared to be volcanic activity of some sort. He recommended suspending attempting any further landing approaches until an aerial survey could determine if there were any safe landing points.

A shocked Admiral Roland had eventually recovered his wits sufficiently to order all ships to stay outside a three mile zone of the landmass and wait for further instructions.

He had then called General Paterson to explain the situation. The General had been hopping mad that he had not been consulted earlier. But soon a mollified General Paterson had understood the gravity of the situation and assured Admiral Roland of his fullest cooperation. Within an hour he would report back to the Admiral with the results of the aerial survey. General Paterson had lost no time in contacting Admiral Tyson and General Garland to set up an emergency meeting. The three of them had quickly worked out a plan to send all available Army, Navy and Air force surveillance planes to check the coastline all around the landmass to identify possible landing points. Within a half hour, fifteen planes equipped with the latest sonar and infrared sensors capable of accurately measuring eddy currents, water temperature, wind velocity and wave motion were surveying the coastline.

It was hopeless. If anything, the eastern side was worse than the western side. Air surveillance had detected vast amounts of what appeared to be molten rock pouring into the Pacific at hundreds of points along the western coast. Infrared patterns showed that the hottest parts measured around 2000 degrees Fahrenheit, and were located adjacent to the submerged portion of the landmass at a depth of 150 to 200 feet. What appeared to be great quantities of steam emerged in vast clouds from several hot spots and vanished without a trace at a depth of about 10 feet. It was conjectured that water vapor emanating from the hot spots gradually condensed on the way up and completely disappeared near the surface. Closer to the surface, at a depth of 2 to 3 feet, they detected many far smaller molten rock streams, barely a trickle compared to the huge volumes gushing out of the larger openings down below. There were no significant steam clouds around these areas and they thought there probably wasn't enough molten rock to vaporize the ocean water in any significant amounts. The surveillance party from the frigate had probably run into one of these. They were so numerous, they were practically unavoidable. The water temperature, even at the surface, was close to boiling point up to a distance of about 150 feet from the shore, and dropped rapidly thereafter.

The situation on the eastern side appeared to be quite different. Great streams of hot gases appeared to be pouring out of massive holes in the side of the submerged landmass at many points along the edge. The jet streams were so strong that they generated eddy currents which even the largest of boats and possibly even the ships would probably not be able to withstand. The hottest spots on this side measured around 800 degrees Farenheit, close to the jet streams emanating from the landmass. They could see a similar kind of vapor cloud pattern, though smaller and less intense, as on the western side. Again, the vapor clouds disappeared as they rose to the surface and no vapor clouds could be detected at depths of around 20 feet. The surface water temperature on the eastern side was about 150 degrees Farenfeit.

It was evident that sea evacuation was impossible. Even more so than evacuation by air. A dejected General Paterson made his promised report to Admiral Roland within an hour. The report sounded like a death knell to Admiral Roland. He issued orders to abandon sea evacuation. All the ships were asked to return to their home bases. A shaken and dispirited Admiral Roland conveyed the news to President Walters. President Walters was devastated. For the first time in his life he felt helpless and completely out of control. He would need time to think it over and see what his options were. Right then, there appeared to be none. But something would emerge.

By a quirk of fate, the doomed sea-evacuation effort had a positive outcome. The aerial survey had generated a wealth of data for the scientists in the special council to analyze. That would provide valuable information.

CHAPTER 7

L ieutenant Strand stood at the head of the large, circular table. Around the table were seated the most eminent group of geologists, geophysicists and seismologists in the land. He didn't know anyone in person. Some he recognized from newspaper pictures and TV interviews. There was Prof. Chambers, the geophysicist from Princeton, Prof. Crompton, the geologist from Harvard, Prof. Gehrich, the seismologist from Caltech. The others he couldn't place. He had the list in front of him. There were 4 geologists, 3 seismologists and 3 geophysicists. Ten in all. Some of them looked red-eyed and weary. The last of them to arrive, Prof. Peterson from Stanford, had come in at 4:00 a.m. It was now 8:00 a.m. About half of them had made it in time for the White House dinner President Walters had hosted for them the previous evening. They had heard a tear-laced account of the disaster from the President himself. The rest, no doubt, would have picked up the details from the others.

"Gentlemen," he said, "I am Lieutenant Strand. President Walters has asked me to coordinate this effort to understand the tragic phenomenon that has wrought this havoc in Southern California. You are all, I am sure, by now aware of the seriousness of the situation. The very survival of the 12 million people on the floating landmass depends on you. We must get some insights into the underlying seismological phenomenon that caused this. We must determine how long the landmass will continue to float, how far it is likely to go, what happens if it collides with another landmass, how stable the landmass is,... a thousand questions. Let us not kid ourselves, these are not easy questions. Given our current knowledge of deep-earth phenomena and the forces that cause them, they are extremely difficult questions to answer. You know that better than I do. Nevertheless, we must do our best. Improvise where we can. Come up with some models that can explain, however crudely, what's going on. It is a desperate situation and the country depends on you. President Walters depends on you. I depend on you. Let me be clear about my role here. You are the experts, I am merely a facilitator. My job is to keep your efforts focused, to make sure you all converge on some meaningful approach. I am sufficiently familiar with continental drift and plate tectonics to know all the controversies surrounding these theories. I know there are many in this room who swear by plate tectonics while there are others who decry it as the greatest hoax. The time has come for us to put aside our scientific differences and concentrate our mental faculties on addressing the situation at hand. Whether you subscribe to plate tectonics theory or not, the fact is that you represent the foremost body of experts on the inner structure of the earth. You represent the best chance these 12 million people have of coming through this. I beg of you, please work together to develop some understanding of this calamity," he paused.

There was a reason for Lieutenant Strand's passionate appeal. He knew how dissent-riven the research community was in this highly specialized branch of science. The theory of continental drift, which claims that all the continents were once held together millions of years ago but gradually drifted apart, dates as far back as Sir Francis Bacon, the famous English philosopher, who observed that the Atlantic coasts of Africa and South America would fit together quite neatly, if juxtaposed. This hypothetical supercontinent was named Panagaea by Alfred Wegener, the first serious proponent of continental drift, in 1915. Wegener argued that the continents separated by virtually breaking through the ocean floors under the influence of some mysterious force. Though Wegener presented a considerable body of evidence in the form of interlocking coastlines, fossils, rocks and glacial remnants in Africa, South America, India and Australia - suggesting that these landmasses were once closer to the South Pole - his inability to explain adequately what great force could have resulted in such large scale drift, led to the rejection of his theory by most scientists in the field. However, in the sixties, a better understanding of the earth's inner structure led to the theory of plate tectonics which provides a remarkable, if not complete, explanation of continental drift.

Present day geologists believe that the earth's interior consists of a solid-rock layer called the lithosphere ranging in thickness from 70 to 350 miles. The lithosphere includes a thin crust, which varies in depth from 3 to 30 miles. Underneath the lithosphere is the hot, rocky mantle going down to a depth of 1800 miles. Below the mantle is the outer core, which is about 1400 miles thick and, at the very center is the inner core, a solid metallic sphere about 750 miles thick. The upper part of the mantle, called asthenosphere, is believed to be a plastic material capable of viscous motion.

The plate tectonics theory argues that the rigid lithosphere is divided into 20 or so plates which float on the asthenosphere much like a wooden log floats on water. This notion that the earth's crust and the lithosphere float on a plastic base is called isostasy and the entire surface of the earth including the continents, the mountains, and the ocean floors, is said to be in isostatic equilibrium. According to the plate tectonics theory, as the oceanic and continental landmasses float, they produce continental drift at the rate of 2 to 10 centimeters per year. The motion of the plates is believed to be due to convectional currents within the hot mantle exerting pressure on the lithosphere. This theory, while providing convincing explanations of phenomena such as earthquakes, volcanoes, creation of island arcs, and so on, had not gained complete acceptance within the scientific community. In fact, eminent scientists had engaged in vitriolic attacks on each other, hurling insults and exchanging diatribes, while the controversy raged on.

Given the bitter divergence of scientific opinion, it was not surprising that Lieutenant Strand was worried about the scientists indulging in their customary petty squabbles instead of focusing on the immediate problem at hand.

"Don't worry Lieutenant," Prof. Chambers, the Princeton geophysicist said, "that won't happen. Prof. Crompton and I actually shook hands." Everybody laughed. It was no secret that the two eminent men were on opposite sides of the plate tectonics camp and had indulged in an exchange of criticism bordering on personal attacks that had become common knowledge within the scientific community. The unexpected quip from an otherwise dead-serious Prof. Chambers, lightened the mood. "In fact," Prof. Chambers continued, "he and I worked all night trying to come up with an explanation, and I think we have a plausible model."

An excited murmur broke out within the group. If the two great men agreed on some common approach, then in all likelihood that would provide a great start.

"If you will allow me Lieutenant, and with the Professor's permission of course," he bowed exaggeratedly to Prof. Crompton, "I will present our idea for consideration by the council."

Lieutenant Strand nodded. He could not have hoped for a better beginning. He turned to Prof. Chambers and said, "That's indeed very encouraging Professor. We would very much like to hear your views. But first, let me share the latest piece of information we got this morning, and after that the floor is yours."

Lieutenant Strand then went on to describe the failed sea-evacuation attempt. When he came to the results of the aerial survey, to the part about jet streams on the eastern coast and molten rock flow on the western coast, Prof. Crompton could not contain himself. He jumped up exclaiming, "By George! Prof. Chambers! Just what we thought, this is incredible!"

Prof. Chambers too was agitated with excitement. They could hardly sit still while Lieutenant Strand finished up. The others felt their excitement and were getting increasingly impatient to hear their theory. Lieutenant Strand summed up in a hurry.

Prof. Chambers stood up and began, "We all know that south western California is rather unique in terms of plate tectonics. It is the only land portion of the otherwise completely oceanic Pacific plate." Everyone nodded. The Pacific plate was one of the 20 odd plates proposed by the plate tectonics theory. "And we know this is where the Pacific plate meets the North American plate to create the famous transform fault, the San Andreas' fault," Prof. Chambers continued. A transform fault was the scientific term for the meeting point of two separate plates,

61

which neither pushed against each other nor pulled apart from each other, but rather, slid past each other. "Now, in theory, at a transform fault junction the two intersecting plates are supposed to slip off each other. But, we know that interlocking masses of rock, at times, resist the sliding motion. The resulting tension build-up and its subsequent release can cause massive earthquakes, like the famous San Francisco earthquake of 1906." All this was well known, it was not clear what the Professor was leading to.

"Here's the interesting proposition. Suppose an earthquake occurred deep under the Pacific floor somewhere off the coast of Southern California. Suppose the focus of the earthquake was so deep down that the surface waves were either not detected or dismissed as one of the numerous microearthquakes that plague that region. Now, we all know that the body waves travel in the interior of the earth. Suppose the body waves traveled all the way to San Andreas' fault and, there, encountering a seismic discontinuity bounced back to interfere constructively with the oncoming body waves. This would be analogous to the behavior of sound waves in wind instruments, except that the wave energy is much greater here. Now, could this not cause vibrations large enough in amplitude to create cracks in the earth's crust under Southern California and perhaps stretching far into the interior of the ocean crust under the Pacific? Now, suppose, by a curious coincidence, the vibrations created cracks in the walls of a large reservoir of natural gas somewhere hitherto unknown, under the Pacific. The gas from this reservoir, possibly under enormous pressure, could rush to fill the cracks, possibly widening the cracks and creating new cracks in the process. Now, suppose the gas rushed to occupy a large, thin, rocky chamber under Southern California. Eventually the pressure could build up to a point where the ignition point was reached and the gas caught fire. Let's conjecture that the intense heat that resulted and the pressure led to a part of the lithosphere melting. This in turn could expose the asthenosphere to the pressure and heat creating a molten mix of magma and hot burning gases, just like in a volcano." Magma was the name given to molten rock and the mix of dissolved gases it contained.

"Except, unlike in a volcano, the mix of magma and burning gases didn't have to push its way upward because of the cracks in the lithosphere already present," an excited Prof. Crompton couldn't help interrupting. The group was listening in rapt attention.

"Yes! Yes! Precisely," Prof. Chambers continued. "And by an even greater coincidence, the lighter gas moved eastward and the magma moved westward towards the ocean, possibly because the cracks created a downward sloping passage towards the ocean which was filled up by the magma forcing the hot gases to flow east towards San Andreas' fault."

"A great deal of hot steam from the magma could have mixed with the gases too!" someone said excitedly. They were all getting drawn into the possibility of what Prof. Chambers was proposing.

"Yes, possibly," Prof. Chambers continued, "now, when the mix of gases and steam under a great deal of pressure reached the San Andeas' fault, a part of the interlocking landmasses snapped, giving way to gigantic blowholes through which the hot gases rushed out like jet streams. The momentum from these jet streams, if sufficiently strong, could rip a part of the crust off. At the same time, the outflow of the jet stream would release the pressure somewhat and cause the dissolved gases in the magma from the asthenosphere to escape under the reduced, by the standards of the mantle, pressure, and mix with the gases already present. This could significantly add to the supply of hot gases in the chamber."

"But wouldn't you expect such a rip closer to the fault than was reported?" someone asked.

"Hard to say. Depends on where the weakest points within the crust are and how far the cracks extended," Prof. Chambers continued. "It is all very plausible so far, but here's where the real speculation starts. The ripped-off crust, for some reason, makes a clean break off the Pacific coast. Perhaps because of some ancient fracture caused by subduction," he paused. Subduction was the process by which the ocean floor caved in and subsided into the crust when an oceanic plate met a continental plate.

"But subduction only occurs at a convergence boundary, and the San Andreas' fault, we all know, is not one," Prof. Gehrich protested. Convergence boundary referred to the meeting of two plates, which push against each other because they are moving in opposite directions.

"I know, I know," Prof. Chambers said patiently, "and this is where plate tectonics stops coming to our rescue. And this is also why Prof. Crompton and I could work together on this. It has successes and failures for plate tectonics. But, just suppose for the time being that for some reason or other the ripped-off crust broke clean from the rest of the lithosphere right off the Pacific coast. Believe me, our anti-tectonics friends will feast on that one for a long time," he was looking at Prof. Crompton. "Now imagine what you have! For all practical purposes a rocketship of unimaginable proportions. A thin crust of earth containing enormous amounts of hot gases and steam under high pressure, the gases rushing out like a jet stream from one end while hot magma pours out at the other. Nature's perfect little, well not so little, rocket! Let's say this rocket begins to slide into the Pacific. Now, why didn't it sink? Because, by another providential coincidence the hot gases have worked their way through the bottom of the ripped off crust creating a multitude of jet streams that gave it enough of a lift to stay afloat! As more and more of the crust slides into the ocean, the ripped-off crust encounters less and less friction between the rocky surfaces and finally breaks loose with a big bang. That could be when the high velocity of 80 miles per hour was reached." Prof. Chambers stopped, sweat was pouring down his face.

"How come severe structural damage didn't occur due to the frictional forces generated when the ripped-off crust was literally dragged on the lithosphere?" Prof. Gehrich challenged.

"Good question," Prof. Crompton said, "could be the mix of gases and magma acted as a lubricant. Could be the ripped-off crust and the lithosphere were semi-molten under the heat and so there wasn't much friction, more like a drag in a highly viscous fluid. The ripped-off crust would have solidified after coming in contact with the ocean water."

"How do you explain the ground caving in under tall buildings and heavy aircraft?" Lieutenant Strand asked.

"Possibly because the isostatic equilibrium was disturbed when the crust was ripped-off and the new equilibrium point reached when the ripped-off crust started to float on the water simply could not support ground pressure beyond a critical threshold," Prof. Chambers said.

His brilliant mind had deduced the sensitivity to pressure distribution on the floating landmass. None of them had, as yet, heard of the KBEE helicopter disaster. When Prof. Chambers heard about it later his scientific mind could not help exulting in the confirmation of his theory provided by that tragedy.

"If you are right about that Prof. Chambers," said Lieutenant Strand, "that floating landmass is extremely unstable. The ground can start caving in at any place, any time." Prof. Chambers just nodded.

"Why did the velocity of the floating landmass slow down to 5 miles per hour later?" someone asked.

"Not really sure," said Prof. Chambers, "but possibly because, with the explosive release of hot gases, the crust moved again and either shut some of the passage ways for the gas, or narrowed them. In either case it would act like a valve closing to reduce the outflow of gases. This would reduce the speed of the jet stream and consequently the speed of the floating landmass which, by the principle of the rocket-engine, must be proportional to the speed of the jet stream."

A lot of questions and discussions followed. How much gas was there? How long would it burn? Would the ground cave in? What would happen if they collided with another landmass? No one knew. Prof. Chambers had a gloomy response to the last question.

"They would probably get buried under collapsing structures before they actually collide. You see, as they approach another landmass, the floating crust would scrape the ocean floor and now it is highly unlikely that they will still have the lubricating effect that saved them when they broke apart. The resulting friction and vibrations will decimate every building," he paused. And then he added, "Unless the slope of the ocean floor is exactly right and the floating landmass fits like a wedge. Imagine the odds of that!"

"Their only chance," added Prof. Gehrich, "is if they get evacuated somehow before they sink or collide. Only God can save them."

Nobody else had a better explanation than the one proposed by Prof. Chambers and Prof. Crompton. Not that they bought into it, it was just that anything else sounded even more unlikely. Someone computed how much gas the floating landmass would need to have just to keep it floating. Somebody else improved the calculations by further figuring out how much more gas they would need to have to make them move at a speed of 5 miles per hour. Another person refined the analysis to estimate the amount of gas needed to keep floating and moving at 5 miles per hour for any specified time duration. All good scientific analysis. But did they actually have that much gas? No one knew.

Lieutenant Strand had grown tired of referring to the floating landmass as breakaway landmass or floating landmass. By the end of the day, his military mind had come up with a suitable acronym.

"Let's call it BLT," he said, "for breakaway landmass terrane." Everyone was amused and agreed it was a good choice. Terrane was the geological term for a series of rock formations, and BLT indeed was a rock formation in a sense. When someone jokingly asked what would happen if BLT ran into The Sandwich Islands, the ensuing mirth ceased abruptly amidst the dark realization that it was indeed a distinct possibility.

CHAPTER 8

*K*ate had trouble falling asleep. She had tossed about for quite a while thinking about the day's events. In a sense her attempts to chase away her personal problems had succeeded. When she returned home after the meeting with General Paterson she hadn't felt as lonely as she had earlier. The break-up with Peter hadn't haunted her to the same degree. True, her thoughts kept going back to him and his Chinese woman. But they had lost their earlier intensity. In fact, she had been surprised to find herself more preoccupied with the events that had transpired in General Paterson's office. She had felt alternately exhilarated and scared at the ruse she had employed to gain the General's audience. That had provided her a vantage position from which to observe, even participate in if she chose to, the relief operations and the evacuation that would surely follow. The thought of that thrilled her. To be at the helm, deciding, making plans, would be a thousand times better than being cooped up in her house, nowhere to go, nothing to do, and not knowing what was going on.

She had correctly sensed the mood of the three military men. They were eager for someone to take control of the civilian affairs, and they would welcome her help. Unless someone in a position of authority, maybe the Mayor of Orange County, or the head of Pacific Aerospace, or some such person showed up, they wouldn't mind if she took over all the civilian responsibilities. Now assuming they let her, should she or shouldn't she? Sooner or later they were bound to find out that she had nothing to do with Mayor Taylor's office. That was the scary part. What would they do to her? Well, what could they do? They had more pressing matters on their minds. They would probably revoke her pass and throw her out. What if she told General Paterson herself first thing in the morning? The effect would be more or less the same. Maybe he would let her continue in some lesser capacity, like assisting the person assuming civilian control, or some such thing. That was not appealing to her at all. She had a shot at running the show. She had to go for it. She would see how the cards played out tomorrow and then decide. She would not wait for them to find out, she would tell them on her own. But first she would wait to see what they had in mind for her. This line of reasoning comforted her and she finally fell asleep, exhausted by the day's events.

When Kate arrived at General Paterson's office at 8:00 next morning, she created quite an impression. She had dressed carefully in her best business suit, smartly tailored to show off her tall, lithe, figure to advantage. Not in a voluptuous or provocative way, but in an attractive, attention-grabbing manner. She looked smart, pretty, feminine and businesslike in a way that intelligent, middle-aged men in powerful positions find irresistible.

Her arrival certainly perked up the glum trio that sat crouched around General Paterson's table. The three men had been in there since 6:00 a.m. The results of the aerial survey had come in only 30 minutes ago and the decision to abandon the sea-evacuation had been taken only a few minutes earlier. They had not yet had time to adjust to the reality of what they had just seen and heard. The disappointment of the failed sea-evacuation attempt was evident on their faces and in their demeanor.

Kate immediately sensed that something had gone terribly wrong. General Paterson briefed her about the failed evacuation attempt and the results of the aerial survey. He told her everything he knew. The President's assurance, the Science Council he had created, everything. At the end of it General Paterson concluded, "Quite simply Miss Upshaw, no evacuation by air or sea is possible. We are stuck on this thing until we either sink or hit a larger landmass, perhaps Hawaii or Asia, and survive the impact. We are quite literally up the proverbial creek without a paddle."

Kate felt an all-consuming feeling of despair overtake her as she listened to the General's description. She must be crazy to want to take control of this mess, she found herself thinking. But when she heard the alternatives, so cogently summed up by General Paterson, she was jolted out of her feeling of hopelessness. What else was there for her to do? Go quietly into the good sea? Not her. She would fight tooth and nail to survive, and to help everyone else survive too.

"Maybe that's my mission," she thought, "maybe that's why God pulled Peter away from me."

Kate was not one to be fatalistic and let other people or events run her life. When her father had deserted them, when her mother had ill-treated them, when she had seen her sisters make the same mistakes one after another, she had emerged stronger, more determined to take control of her own life. To make it better. She was going to do the same now. Bend as the wind blows. Especially if they are winds of change. Even more so if they are typhoons of change.

Kate had been so absorbed with her own thoughts that she hadn't spoken or shown any external reaction to

General Paterson's description. So she was startled when she heard Admiral Tyson say, "Well, Miss Upshaw, what do you think? What are our options?"

She found herself saying without any conscious thought, "Admiral, now that we know where we stand, we should not waste any time. Hopefully, the President's Science Council will soon tell us what this phenomenon is all about, how long we can keep floating, what's the probability of colliding with Hawaii, or Asia, or Australia, or whatever. The important thing is that we must assume that we are going to be floating as long as we need to, and act on that assumption. Now that we are going to be here for a while, we should first get a good picture of what we have on our hands. The most important is the communications network. We have to fix the phone network right away. Radio, TV and satellite can wait. We must check on the food and water situation. Power is important too. We haven't had power supply in almost a day. To pull this off we need the right resources. It will take time to mobilize the civilian resources. I think we should start with all available military resources. What do you think?" She was addressing all three of them.

All three of them nodded. They all had the same thought running through their minds. She was young, smart, and had the drive to succeed. They couldn't have found a better person to take over. She maybe short on experience, but they could make up for that. When General Paterson spoke, he voiced all their thoughts.

"Miss Upshaw," he said, "between the Army, Air Force and Navy bases here, we probably have around 400 trained communications experts. I am going to propose to General Garland and Admiral Tyson that we create a common

71

communications team headed by Karl Johnson who commands the Army Communications Corps. Under Karl's leadership, this team can take care of the communications networks. I suspect food will not be a problem. Southern California is one of the few places in the U.S. that is completely self sufficient in terms of food. Water maybe a problem. As I recall, we get a significant portion of our water from the north. Power will definitely be a problem. Most of our power comes from the power grids fed by the Hoover Dam. That's something we have to monitor. Between the Army, Air Force and Navy, we must have enough electrical engineers who can assess the situation and recommend the best solution. None of these issues really worries me. I am confident that we can handle them." He paused to check their reaction. General Garland and Admiral Tyson were nodding agreement. "What really bothers me is this: how are we going to communicate the news regarding the situation we are in to 10 million people. We've got to tell them the bad news, convey the seriousness of it, in such a way that they understand the hopelessness of it, but yet they should not panic. They should believe that we are in control and everything that is possible is being done. We've got to find a person who can get this message across to them. I don't believe any of us can do it," he was pointing to Admiral Tyson and General Garland. "People just don't have that kind of trust in the military any more. This is where you come in. In the absence of Mayor Taylor, you would be the logical choice. What do you think?"

Kate was stunned. Even though this is what she had been hoping for, the suddenness of it had taken her by surprise. "There are lots of other mayors you could pick from," she said, "why me? I have no experience in this kind of thing."

"The other mayors just don't have the stature Mayor Taylor has. We all know that the Mayor of LA is the political bigwig around here. Others don't even come close. By virtue of being his press secretary, you would have pretty high credibility," General Paterson said.

"I agree, if we can't locate Mayor Taylor, I think you should be our spokesperson," Admiral Tyson endorsed General Paterson's opinion.

"I agree," General Garland pitched in.

"I would like some time to think it over. How would I go about addressing the people any way?" Kate asked.

General Paterson seemed to have thought through all the answers. "I have a plan," he said, "let's split our communications team into two groups. Let one half worry about the phone network. The other half will focus on the cable TV network. Practically all the houses have cable. If we get the cable stations working and if we fix at least one of the TV stations, we will have a pretty good TV network going. I am sure we have at least one TV station here on this piece of land. Once we have the TV network up and running you can appear on TV and address the people. If you all agree, I'll ask Karl to set the plan in motion."

It seemed to make sense. Everybody agreed. A joint communications team under Karl's command was set up. General Paterson arranged for Kate to have an office next to his.

"It makes sense for you to stay here so you can stay plugged in. If not, it'll be a nuisance having to brief you on all the little details," he said. In his mind, it was a foregone conclusion that Kate would address the people and assume responsibility for all civilian matters. Some kind of a makeshift government would have to be formed. He didn't want to scare Kate with the details, but that's what he was thinking.

He needn't have worried. Kate's brain was already buzzing. The amorphous notion of a makeshift government that General Paterson had been thinking of had taken a concrete form in her mind. Alone in her new office, she was thinking what kind of a government it would be. She couldn't possibly be formally elected. They just didn't have the infrastructure to hold elections. Maybe General Paterson could propose her as the head of the government and people could call in, once their phones were working, to vote yes or no. If she got a majority, she would take control. If not, someone else could have a shot at it. Would they call themselves a city, a county, or a state? City or county would imply that they were part of some state. They would never again be a part of California. With some luck, a lot of luck actually, they could collide with some landmass in Hawaii, or Asia or Australia, or whatever. The best they could hope for would be to continue to be a part of the United States. It would make sense then to consider themselves a state. The fifty-first state. The idea thrilled her in a strange way. She would be the governor then. Governor Kate. No, too informal. Governor Upshaw. Had a nice ring to it. She could not contain her excitement. She had lost track of the fact that both she, and her hopes, could sink any minute.

What would she have to worry about as governor? She would need to appoint the state cabinet. She would need a defense secretary, an education secretary, someone to keep track of all the communications networks, power, and so on. That could be the science and technology secretary. She would need a health and sanitation secretary, of course. What about the treasury secretary? That would have to wait. It was not clear what source of revenue they would have. Could people be taxed in a situation like this? Not many would be working in the near future. She was not, herself. So they wouldn't be getting paid. Which meant no income taxes. They could hardly pay for anything, which meant no sales taxes. She suddenly realized that all they needed was a distribution system to distribute food, water, power, everything. Most people wouldn't be able to pay for anything. It would have to be plain and simple goodwill. Those who had resources would share it. Those who wished to work in any capacity would volunteer. For the foreseeable future that was the only system that would work. No one could be coerced into doing anything against their will. Not after the condition they would be reduced to once they learned about the situation they were in. A spirit of camaraderie brought about by a sense of shared misfortune was their only hope. That was it! She would call it The State of Good Hope. Because that was all they really had, good hope. That was the only currency they could trade in. If, and when, they achieved permanent stability, they would receive federal assistance, of course. President Walters would surely be generous. That would put their economy back on track. She would surely need a treasury secretary then. But first they would have to worry about survival. They could only achieve that through cooperation. Cooperation on a scale unheard of in modern history. It had to be almost a perfect mixture of democracy, socialism and communism working in harmony. Certainly not capitalism. There was no room for it. Capitalism would be anathema. She was startled to realize that the most elemental aspect of America, the very essence of American life-style, what was ingrained into every American since birth, capitalism, would have to be forsaken. Capitalism was a luxury they could not afford. If they were a private company, their stock would be worth nothing on Wall Street. Nothing.

Inspired by her thoughts, she sat down to write her speech, the one she would have to make when she addressed the people on TV. She would have to go beyond merely communicating the situation, as General Paterson had indicated. Well beyond. She would have to inculcate hope in the people. And faith. She would have to outline the form the government would take. A government truly for the people and by the people, in a way that Lincoln couldn't possibly have foreseen. She would have to persuade the people to believe in her plan. To participate. This was the only chance she would get. If she failed to capitalize on the sense of shock her announcement of their situation would create, then the failure would not be hers alone, but of all the people. It was unlikely that anyone else, even Mayor Taylor, would succeed, once cynicism and desperation set in. Fear leading to optimism leading to a deep sense of sharing was their only chance.

She had no trouble writing her speech. In a little under three hours, she had the whole speech written and memorized. She felt so intensely about it, she had memorized it, word for word, as she wrote, with no effort at all.

After she finished writing her speech, she had nothing to do. She went to the lounge to see what was on TV. She flipped through the channels. Predictably, they were all covering the Southern California disaster. The same scenes, the same words. Shots of the Pacific splashing against a cliff on which stood what was left of downtown LA. Shots of water covering what was once the Southwestern part of California. Shots of dazed people, sunken buildings, rescue operations. Estimates of loss. Aerial shots of the breakaway landmass. Discussion of their fate. Theories about earthquakes and volcanoes. Possible evacuation attempts. Apparently no one on the mainland knew about the aborted evacuation-by-sea effort.

Kate watched, fascinated at first, particularly by the incongruous sight of downtown LA aloft on its perch. The sheer, jagged edges created by the breakaway landmass looked raw like fresh wounds. But soon she found her thoughts drifting. She found it impossible to focus on the screen. Their own situation was so ridiculous, so utterly hopeless, that the images on the TV paled in comparison. At least they were together, connected. Their needs being attended to. Not adrift like some jettisoned waste. Moving without direction. Floating at the whim of some strange, unknown, phenomenon. With each passing moment, she felt herself growing more and more remote, disconnected from the scenes on TV. Why should she care what they thought? They could do nothing for her.

She felt a flicker of interest when she saw Mayor Taylor being interviewed. He was back in LA promising its citizens quick and painless reunification with their separated loved ones. He was personally guaranteeing that Southern California would be whole again. Even if they had to haul the separated landmass piece by piece. The man had no clue what he was talking about. He was just telling the people what they wanted to hear. Kate felt disgusted at the Mayor's blatant self-aggrandizement.

Watching Mayor Taylor on TV, Kate had a sudden realization. It was likely that her speech would be beamed via satellite to the mainland. Someone there would know that she was not Mayor Taylor's press secretary. In fact, someone here was bound to know. Stupid of her not to have thought about it. She decided then and there that she would ask General Paterson not to introduce her as Mayor Taylor's press secretary. And she would tell him who she really was. Right after the speech.

Around 6:00 p.m. General Paterson sent for Kate. Karl Johnson, the chief of the Army Communications Corps, had returned. He had brought back good news. The task of getting the TV network up and running had proceeded more smoothly than anticipated. They only had to fix the satellite dishes at the cable stations and orient them towards the antenna at the TV station. They had repaired the antenna at KLAN TV station, Channel 11, and checked to make sure that all the cable stations could receive the signal. They hadn't had any problem. The cables running from the cable station to the residential areas had been more troublesome. Many of them had been cut. They had to painstakingly test each cable, determine which ones needed repair and had to send technicians to track down the problem and fix it. Fortunately, they had received help from the cable company technicians who had seen the military technicians poking about cable boxes around their homes and had offered to help. That had been a great relief. More than half the cables had been fixed. Karl figured that by noon the next day they would have fixed all repairable cables. Some of the problems would be trickier to identify and repair. He estimated that some 90 percent of the households would be part of the restored cable TV network by noon. In fact, Karl felt that if they ran a feed from the steerable antenna in the Army base to the TV station, then these 90 percent of the households could receive all of the national TV channels from the mainland.

The news on the telephone network front was mixed. Of the 220 switches on the breakaway landmass, 78 were seriously damaged, mostly because they were housed in tall buildings that had sunk. Some of these could possibly be fixed if they replaced broken parts with spares from military stocks. Others were damaged beyond repair and would have to be replaced. He didn't think they could obtain any replacement switches. All houses and businesses directly connected to the broken switches would be without phone service. It was quite possible that even those with restored phone service would not be able to reach some parts of the landmass, because of breaks in the network. They would not know until the fiber optic cables connecting the switches were fixed. About half of the residential phone lines connecting the switches to the phones at home appeared to be damaged too. They would need to be repaired as well. He was not sure how long that would take. He expected quite a few to be operational by the end of the next day. Power would be restored by morning, but the power situation was grim. The local generators would not be able to sustain normal power consumption. They would have to impose some form of rationing.

General Paterson was pleased on the whole. He felt they should not delay the TV address any more than necessary. They all agreed to meet with Karl again at 11:30 a.m. the next day to assess the situation. If Karl's expectation was correct and most of the houses had TV service restored, then they would schedule the TV address for 7:00 p.m. They would send military trucks equipped with loudspeakers to every nook and corner of the landmass to announce to the people that most of them had access to KLAN, Channel 11. To spread the message that KLAN was up and running, they would get KLAN to show one of the Hollywood classics. Admiral Tyson had suggested 'Gone With the

Wind' or 'Citizen Kane'. Kate found herself hoping that KLAN would choose 'Gone With the Wind'. The great classic would not only lift the spirits of the people, obvious parallels between her and Scarlet O'Hara would be drawn. Besides, the conclusion of the movie with Scarlet O'Hara saying "Tomorrow is another day," would be the perfect lead-in to her speech.

CHAPTER 9

*W*hen they met with Karl the next day at 11:30 a.m., they found him as good as his word. All the TV cables that could be easily repaired had been fixed. The others would take time. Karl estimated that somewhere around 80 percent to 90 percent of the households had TV restored. Just one channel, but that was one more than they had had, and provided a crucial means of mass communication. They were pleasantly surprised to learn that about half of the phone network was up and running. Roughly half of the households would have working phones, though they may not all be able to talk to each other. Power had been restored, but they would have to start rationing soon.

General Paterson immediately swung into action. He had already talked to the President of KLAN and persuaded him to go along with their plan. He now called him to confirm it. When he got off the phone he turned to Kate smiled and said "Get ready for your first TV appearance Miss Upshaw, you are on."

Kate felt a momentary sense of panic. She thought of her speech and that gave her confidence. She looked at General Paterson and said, "Thank you General. I am ready. But....I have a request," she paused. All three men were looking intently at her. "I would like you not to introduce me as the Mayor's press secretary."

"Look here, Kate," General Paterson said sharply. He stopped abruptly, embarrassed. "I am sorry Miss Upshaw," he continued. His voice had lost its edge. "I didn't mean it, it was a slip."

"Quite all right General. In fact, I would like all three of you to call me Kate," Kate said.

"OK Kate," General Paterson continued, "what I meant to say was, the public needs to know you have some official standing to attach credence to your announcement. I feel strongly that linking you to Mayor Taylor's office will give your words more weight."

Kate was in a spot. She didn't know how to counter General Paterson. It took her just a few seconds to come up with one of her inspired improvisations.

"General," she said, "I understand what you are saying. I would have liked that too. But after what I saw on TV yesterday, I don't feel like linking myself to Mayor Taylor's office, I find the very idea repugnant." She proceeded to describe to them the statements Mayor Taylor had made on TV. She liberally embellished what she had seen and painted Mayor Taylor as a self-serving opportunist more interested in generating political capital out of their plight, than in their well being.

"Has any one of you gotten a call from the Mayor?" she asked, addressing all of them. They all shook their heads. "There, proves my point. Goes to show how sensitive he is to our needs. He is too busy enjoying the limelight to worry about us. He's probably figured that we don't matter any more as far as his votebank is concerned." She could see that all three were upset at what they heard.

General Paterson thought about it for a while and then he said, "Kate, I appreciate your sentiments. I understand why you would want to distance yourself from Mayor Taylor. But in order to expedite..."

Kate didn't let him finish. "That's precisely the point General," she said, "expediency. Mayor Taylor is doing what's politically expedient for him. And I would be doing the same by invoking his name. I absolutely refuse to do it." Her voice was firm.

General Paterson shrugged his shoulders. "Well, OK," he said, "if you want to make your job harder, that's your choice. Make sure your speech hits home. It's now even more important."

Kate was thrilled, she had won temporary reprieve. She would have to tell them, of course. First thing after the speech, she decided. Something was gnawing at the back of her mind. She had been so quick to lie. And so often too. With no conscious thought. Was it her public persona emerging? She better watch out. She liked the old Kate, honest and reliable. She didn't want to lose her. "No more," she said to herself, "I don't care what it costs."

KLAN had told General Paterson that they planned to show 'Gone With The Wind'. They would start the movie at 3:00 p.m. and finish a little before 7:00 p.m. Kate's address would be right after the movie. General Paterson took care of the arrangements for making the announcement about the TV address. Hundreds of Army trucks equipped with PA systems were dispatched. Each truck had a driver and a sergeant with specific instructions and a precisely worded announcement. The announcement said, "Ladies and gentlemen, this is a message from General Paterson of the U.S. Army, Southern California Command. We have an important announcement. As you all know, we are the victims of a terrible earthquake. Please do not panic, the situation is under control. General Paterson has personally taken charge of the situation. Your safety and well being are his foremost concern. The Army, Air Force, and Navy have been working round the clock to restore TV, phone, and power. Most homes now have TV. Some have phone service. Power has been restored. General Paterson will address you all at 7:00 p.m. today to brief you of the situation and to tell you what he is doing about it. Please tune into Channel 11, KLAN, to watch the address. Repeat, tune into Channel 11 at 7:00 p.m. for General Paterson's address. Channel 11 will show a movie starting at 3:00 p.m. for your enjoyment. The address will immediately follow the movie."

Kate was getting ready to leave. She wanted to go back to her house, rest awhile and return dressed appropriately to make a good impression on her TV audience. She told General Paterson that she would meet him at the KLAN studio at 6:30 p.m. General Paterson wouldn't hear of her driving back by herself. He insisted on sending one of his personal staff to drive her home and to bring her back to the studio. Before she left, he asked Kate, "Kate, do you have your speech, can I see it?"

Kate had the speech tucked away in her purse. She said, "Don't worry General, this one's from the heart. I don't need to write it down."

When they reached home, it was a quarter to four. Kate made coffee for her and the sergeant who drove her. She had been looking forward to watching 'Gone With The Wind'. She sat down to watch for a little while and was soon completely engrossed. She had seen the movie several times before, but had never felt its intensity the way she did now. She had been right, the beautiful Scarlet

O'Hara fighting against all odds for the survival of those who depended on her, would set just the right mood. When she realized it was close to half past five, she rushed to get dressed. She had just half an hour, they would have to leave at 6:00. She dressed carefully. She chose a long green velvet dress open at the neck, but not too deep. A pearl necklace to set off her lovely, slender, throat. Her hair rolled up, to give her a simple, elegant, look. A green purse to match and green shoes. Not too much makeup, she didn't want a painted look.

When she returned to the family room shortly before 6:00, she looked strikingly beautiful. The sergeant couldn't help expressing his admiration. "You look lovely miss," he said. Kate was pleased.

It was a little past 6:30 when she got to the TV studio. General Paterson was waiting for her. He saw Kate and nodded approvingly. They were taken to the lounge to wait for the movie to end.

The movie ended at 6:55. The studio staff had alerted them at 6:45. The make-up man had touched both of them up. They had gone over the plan once. General Paterson would be introduced by the evening news anchorman. General Paterson would make a short statement, introduce Kate and leave the floor to her. It would then be Kate's show. They had nothing else planned, so she could take as long as she liked.

When the movie ended, Kate's face had tear streaks. She had been caught up in it again. The make-up man had to touch her up quickly. As they walked to the studio floor Kate was saying to herself, "Move over Scarlet O'Hara, it's now Kate Upshaw to the rescue."

It was a simple studio setting. At the center was a table behind which the anchorman sat, awaiting them. Two chairs on the other side of the table and a podium with a microphone. Kate remained in the background while the anchorman introduced General Paterson. General Paterson was very businesslike and matter of fact. No trace of emotions.

"Ladies and gentlemen," he said, "you are all aware of the tragedy that has befallen us. General Garland and Admiral Tyson, my colleagues from the Air Force and Navy, and I, have been working with Miss Kate Upshaw to assess the situation and to plan the relief operations. As you are already aware, TV service has been restored substantially, telephone service partially, and power completely. We are, even now, working to make things smoother and this disaster more endurable. We have placed Miss Kate Upshaw in charge of coordinating all civilian operations. I would now like to present Miss Upshaw to provide you further details."

Kate walked to the floor, the very picture of repose and self-confidence. She shook hands with the General and walked over to the podium. When she stood behind the podium facing the cameras, she had, without quite realizing it, assumed a regal countenance. She looked like a perfect combination of Margaret Thatcher and Audrey Hepburn.

"Thank you General," she said, and continued, "friends, every so often in the history of humankind an event occurs that changes the very character of the people impacted by it. For many generations to come, such an event will continue to define and guide the peoples' behavior. The exodus from Egypt must have been so for the Jewish people. The Jews in Egypt were exploited and enslaved and desperately needed a way out. So Moses parted the Red Sea to make way for the Jews, to let them escape. Now, for some reason not yet apparent to us, God has cast us into the Pacific so that we may make our way to the destination He has in mind for us. As you know, at 10:30 a.m. yesterday, we experienced what appeared to be a pretty strong earthquake. Approximately an hour later something stranger happened. A 200-mile stretch of Southern California was ripped off the U.S. mainland and thrust into the Pacific Ocean. We don't know as yet why. All we know is that we are now floating somewhere in the Pacific, about 350 miles from the California coast." She paused. She could imagine the look of consternation and disbelief on the faces of millions of people listening to her.

"Before you panic and curse your fate, let me hasten to add that we are the lucky ones. At least we are alive. Not many of the people in what is left of Southern California survived. There has been large-scale casualties and destruction of property. The force that tore us off the mainland was so strong that it nearly leveled the rest of Southern California. That's small consolation to us, though. We don't know much about the phenomenon that caused this extensive damage. We do know that at the moment of separation we were thrown into the Pacific at a very high speed. About 80 miles per hour. We are currently moving at approximately 5 miles per hour. We are in no immediate danger. We are in touch with Washington via the military satellites. President Walters and the Governor of California have personally called to express sympathy and support. They have pledged to do whatever is humanly possible to help us survive this disaster. President Walters has set up a scientific team consisting of the best experts in America to understand the phenomenon that caused this. Their preliminary findings are that we will continue to float for a long period of time and we are in no danger of sinking."

There she was improvising again, creating a seamless blend of fact and fiction. They had, in fact, not received any news after the aborted sea-evacuation attempt, and this had been a source of great concern to all of them. But her job was to alleviate their anxiety, not to aggravate it.

Kate continued with her address, "I can well imagine how you feel at this very moment. Shattered, confused, scared, helpless, your faith destroyed. Believe me, you have every right to be. General Paterson, General Garland, Admiral Tyson and I went through the same emotions yesterday. And now, more than 24 hours later, the tumult in my mind has not subsided. It is in fact this very emotional upheaval that has prompted me to join our military leaders to provide them civilian support. I, like you, am an ordinary citizen, scared and confused by this cataclysmic event. I want to make sure that I reflect your feelings and concerns in the joint effort we must undertake to determine our fate.

"You all know that we lost power, TV, and telephone service. Some people have no water. There have been fires. Many tall buildings have collapsed. Over a thousand people have died. Many more are injured, quite a few seriously. But this is not all. It gets worse than this." Her voice was breaking and she had to brush back her tears.

"I want you all to brace yourself for what I am about to tell you. Parents, I urge you to control your reactions so as not to frighten your children. Remember, they understand even less of this than we do, and they react to our reactions. So for their sake, please be calm. Our floating landmass appears incapable of sustaining any concentration of pressure. All heavy aircraft in all of our airports have sunk into the ground. This is probably why the taller buildings sank as well. This means we cannot be evacuated by air. The only aircraft that can fly in and out of here are helicopters and small planes. We cannot possibly evacuate the 10 to 12 million or so of us stuck on this landmass, using small aircraft. Therefore, President Walters decided that the best alternative was to evacuate us by sea. So he had a large fleet of ships sail here to take us back. But, unfortunately, God has willed otherwise. They found it impossible to approach us by sea. On the western side, thousands of tons of molten rock are pouring into the ocean. The temperature of this molten rock is about 2000 degrees Fahrenheit and it is hot enough to burn or melt any material it comes in contact with. The eastern side has powerful jets of gas streaming out of the landmass creating currents that even our largest ships cannot endure. As a result, evacuation by sea is not possible, either. We are all essentially stuck on a huge, gigantic, rudderless ship moving God only knows where. It is clear that we cannot steer this ship by any physical or mechanical means. It is our collective faith alone that will see us through," she paused to have a drink of water.

"Forgive me if I have painted a picture of utter hopelessness. That is not my intention. We must all have the true picture of the situation we are in. We must face up to the sheer magnitude of the calamity that has struck us. This does not, however, mean that we simply throw up our hands and await our fate. A sense of realism and the collective will to combat adversity will sustain us through this. Now that we all know where we stand, let me share with you my thoughts on what we can do.

"We must begin by changing our attitudes, our values, our biases and prejudices, our immediate ambitions and aspirations. In short, we must leave behind life as we knew it. That was fine yesterday. But this is today. We cannot get in our cars and drive to work. There is no work. We are simply a community of 10 million people floating in the middle of the Pacific, just trying to survive. We are all in it together. We, quite literally, will sink or sail together. It does not matter if you are rich or poor, black or white, Jewish or Christian. We are simply people cast into the ocean by forces more powerful than anything known to man. You may believe in God, you may not. You maybe an atheist, or an agnostic. It is immaterial. It simply does not matter. What matters is this: we must marshall our resources, instill a deep sense of cooperation unknown to modern man. Replace individual drives by an overwhelming sense of the common good. I know this is hard. It is hard for me too. It goes against our grain, our values, and our upbringing. But our collective will must prevail. All our energies must be devoted to a single purpose - to stay afloat until we strike another landmass, or until the flow of molten rock subsides and sea evacuation becomes possible. Let me reiterate. We must give up our sense of the Individual, the family, the neighborhood, and gather all 10 million of us into a common fold. Pool our resources and cooperate so that we may all survive. The alternative is that we all perish; some may die poor, some rich; some young, some old; some black, some white; but succumb we all will. The only way to give ourselves a fighting chance is to create a foundation of hope and faith on which a structure of sharing and cooperation can be built and through which we can offer each other sustenance and endurance.

"We will need some kind of government to coordinate all this. Not a government in the usual non-participative, apathetic sense that most of us have come to view it. This must truly be a government of the people, by the people, and for the people, in a way the great Lincoln himself could not have imagined. It must be a government that simply gives a form to the structure of hope, faith, sharing and cooperation that I was alluding to, and which lets people participate voluntarily and to the best of their abilities. There can be no enforcement or coercion, but a simple spirit of voluntary sharing of labor and resources.

"I have given some thought to what government structure is appropriate for the circumstances we are in. Let me share my thoughts with you. Think of this as a proposal. If we all agree, let's go ahead according to my plan. If not, let's come up with something better. It seems to me that our most important task is to repair the damages wrought by this phenomenon, so we can go about our lives as normally as possible. I suggest we have a Secretary of Relief Operations to oversee this. Next in priority order is the job of ensuring an adequate supply of basic essentials like food, water, and so on. I suggest we create the position of a Secretary of Civil Supplies for this. Third, we must ensure that a communications network, including telephone, radio and TV is available to us at all times. This is absolutely essential, a medium of communication to share our thoughts and maintain a dialog is a must for our survival. I propose the position of Secretary of Science and Technology for this purpose. This same office will also be responsible for monitoring the availability of energy resources like gas, electricity and so on. We don't have a firm handle on the situation regarding energy. We may need to regulate energy use and ration it, we must be prepared for it. We should continue with the law enforcement structure as it was before. I pray and hope that we won't need it, but we must be realistic. I am not sure if the LAPD commissioner is with us or not. If he is not, the highest-ranking officer of the LAPD who is here with us can take control of law enforcement. In the same vein, we will need a justice department. I suggest that the existing structure continue and we appoint a

Chief Justice. Lastly, defense. We must remember that we are afloat in the middle of nowhere. We can rely on our national defense forces to protect us. But considering how far away we are from the mainland, we must be prepared to defend ourselves. Fortunately for us, we have three very capable leaders in General Paterson, General Garland and Admiral Tyson, the chiefs of the Army, Air Force and Navy, respectively. I propose we create the position of a Defense Secretary to formally coordinate our military forces. This may become important, if and when we drift into less friendly parts of the Pacific. Remember that Southern California has the most advanced military aircraft and missile systems manufacturing capabilities in the world and we don't want unfriendly governments casting greedy eyes on us.

"As you will no doubt have noticed, there is no Treasury Secretary or Income Tax Department, or any such thing. I do not feel they are needed. For the foreseeable future, we will have no revenues, no income, no taxes whatsoever. As I have repeatedly said, the only way we can pull this off is by sharing our resources. Everything we have must be shared. Our money has no value. Our homes, food, clothing, everything must be shared. Those who have will give to those who do not. Those who are able, will work. How are we going to enforce all this, you may ask. We will not, because we cannot. It will work on a purely voluntary basis. That is why the realization that we are all in it together and our very survival depends on complete cooperation is of the utmost importance.

"Finally, I would like to say a few words on what identity we should give ourselves. We are no doubt Americans. But we are temporarily dislocated. We are experiencing something remarkable and unprecedented which the rest of our compatriots on the mainland, are not. I feel it is important to give ourselves an identity that creates a common bond. Should we call ourselves a county, a town, a city? Any of these would imply that we are part of some state. Which state? Certainly not California. We are irrevocably and forever, separated from California. God willing, we will return to California soon, but not as this particular body of people brought together by a particular set of unique circumstances. I feel that we can truly only consider ourselves to be a part of America. No matter where we end up, we will be Americans, and eventually, I hope, return to America. I, therefore, propose that we declare ourselves a state, The State of Good Hope. We will, of course, need ratification by the Congress and Senate. Perhaps a constitutional amendment is needed. But given our extraordinary circumstances, they should support us. With your permission, I would like to offer to serve as the first Governor of The State of Good Hope. Why me, you may wonder. Not because I have any experience in office. I do not. I just have the deep desire to channel our collective energies to fight for our survival. All I can offer is my enthusiasm, dedication and willingness to work until my last breath. But it is not important that I should be Governor. If somebody more experienced wants to step up, all the better. What is important is that we consider the proposal before us and evaluate the pros and cons objectively and come to a rational decision. What I am asking for is a radical departure from our familiar paradigm, so before you embark on it you must carefully weigh it and convince yourself that it is worthwhile. No, let me go one step further, you must convince yourself that it is the only option before us. If you have the slightest doubt, please discard my proposal. For it will only work if you all believe in it.

"I would like to conclude this address with a final note of caution. Judging from the collapse of tall buildings and the sinking of large aircraft, it appears that our landmass cannot support any weight beyond a certain critical threshold. I urge you all not to congregate in large numbers. Please do not have large meetings at schools, churches, municipal buildings, anywhere for that matter. I suggest that all schools remain closed until we have a better grasp of the situation.

"I spoke longer than I intended to. I beg your forgiveness if I have shocked, angered or confused you. God bless us all." She stopped, exhausted. She had a giddy sensation. She barely noticed the loud applause from General Paterson and the studio staff.

General Paterson walked over to Kate and hugged her, not realizing they were still on the air. His eyes were moist. "Kate, you were simply wonderful. Sensational," he said. "Did you come up with all this on your own? This is simply incredible."

Kate didn't say anything. She couldn't speak. General Paterson wanted Kate to join him for dinner in his office. "Let's discuss some details," he said. Kate accepted.

On the way back, while General Paterson was still gushing forth on how cogent, articulate, sympathetic yet realistic she had been, Kate waited for an opportune moment and said, "General, I have a confession to make."

At first General Paterson thought she was apologizing for not taking him into her confidence, regarding the proposal she made on TV. "Don't worry, Kate," he said, "I am not offended that you didn't talk to me first about the proposal. To tell you the truth, I was in the beginning. Not any more. You had to sound spontaneous to be convincing. And that you were."

"It is not that General, it is something else."

"What else could be bothering you? Go ahead, tell me."

"I lied to you about being Mayor Taylor's press secretary. I have nothing to do with Mayor Taylor. I am an architect." She proceeded to tell him about how she had felt the urge to find more information and to see if she could help, how she had lied to the guard at the base to get in and how she had found it convenient to let the lie continue to gain access to the General.

The General was aghast.

"I hope you will forgive me General. I am not like that. I am honest and straightforward. I really am. But I felt so helpless, not knowing what was going on. Still, I shouldn't have lied to you." She began to sob uncontrollably. The strain of the speech and the emotions she had stirred in her audience and herself, had been too much for her.

General Paterson put his arm around her. "Kate, listen," he said in a soft voice, "you meant well. That's what matters. God alone knows the real truth. For us, mere mortals, it is the motivation and intent that matter. By that measure, you did not lie. That's good enough for me."

"You mean you won't do anything about it?" Kate asked, disbelieving.

"Of course I will. I intend to do everything I can, possibly," General Paterson was smiling. "I will have to discuss with General Garland and Admiral Tyson, but I don't expect they will object. Not after your speech tonight.

No, they won't. I want to deploy 10000 troops to conduct a door-to-door opinion poll. A simple questionnaire: 'Did you like Kate Upshaw's proposal? Yes or No. Do you want Kate Upshaw to be Governor? Yes or No. And by God, if you don't get 80 percent of the people saying yes to both, I'll resign." He added a moment later, "Resign from what, I don't know. I am no longer sure of what I am. But, Kate, whatever I am, count on my support. And don't think I am flattering you. I am not. We need you for our survival. If anyone can pull this one off, it is you."

CHAPTER 10

*T*hree days later The State of Good Hope was born. The fifty-first state. Created by a special amendment to the constitution. Both Congress and the Senate had passed the bill in record time and President Walters had signed it. Kate Upshaw had become the youngest governor in the United States. President Walters had personally called to congratulate her. So had the Governor of California, the Mayor of LA, many heads of state, countless others. The president of KLAN had had the brilliant idea of broadcasting Kate's speech to the mainland. He had talked to General Paterson about beaming the signal via the Army steerable antenna to an Army satellite and from there to CNN for broadcasting all over the U.S. General Paterson had agreed enthusiastically. He had thought that the speech would make a terrific impact.

Even he had underestimated the impact Kate's speech would have on the American people. For that matter, on the whole world. CNN had first aired the speech only within the continental U.S. But the response had been so overwhelming that CNN decided to broadcast the speech on its international network. Within 24 hours the speech was seen in every single country where CNN had a presence. CNN estimated that 3.5 to 4 billion people had seen it all over the world, making it by far the most watched event on TV. Kate Upshaw had become the most famous person in the world.

Within The State of Good Hope, the response to Kate's speech had been nothing short of incredible. It had taken General Paterson's men two days to cover the approximately 3 million households in The State of Good Hope. 95 percent of the adults polled were in favor of Kate's proposal and over 90 percent wanted her to be the governor. Kate had been moved to tears when General Paterson had given her the numbers.

"General," she had said, "this is scary, I don't know if I can live up to their expectations."

"Nonsense Kate," the General had replied, "whenever you are in doubt just watch your tape and you'll inspire yourself. You can do it."

And, in fact, Kate had secretly followed his advice. She had obtained a copy from KLAN and watched it and come away feeling confident.

The day after Kate's speech, KLAN had received thousands of calls from people expressing support and volunteering help. The KLAN staff had gotten into the spirit of things and organized themselves into a small band of people to receive the calls, note down the important numbers and pass them on to Kate and General Paterson. Practically all of Kate's cabinet had been chosen from that list.

Kate had prepared a short-list and personally contacted everyone on the short-list and asked them to submit their resume. She had then gone through the resumes with General Paterson and invited three people for each position, to attend an interview. She and the General had then carefully questioned each interviewee to determine their suitability for the particular job. When Kate had been over insistent on hiring a person with the right qualification, General Paterson had lost his temper.

"Screw the qualifications Kate!" he had said, "no one on earth is qualified in a situation like this. Go with your gut feeling. Conviction, that's what you need. Look at you! You are not qualified. But you are motivated. And you have conviction. You want to do the right thing and you can persuade people to believe in you. That's what counts. That's what you need, more of you. That'll be hard. Look for lesser reflections of your own self, and you'll do fine."

Kate had been simultaneously angry and flattered, but the message had gotten across. She and the General had assembled a pretty good bunch. They had chosen Frank Jewell, the president of Pacific Aerospace, for the Secretary of Defense. General Paterson knew him personally and thought very highly of him.

"No one knows more about defense than Frank," General Paterson had said. "Knows every fighter aircraft, every guided missile made in Southern California. Could have been the Defense Secretary to any of the previous three presidents, had he chosen to. But liked his job too much, I guess. I think he really feels it is important for him to participate now, that must be why he wants this job. Take him."

Kate had consented. She had by then seen enough of General Paterson to realize that he had very high standards and he was very discerning. They had chosen Gail Warland, the administrator of the largest hospital in Southern California, as the secretary of Relief Operations. Dr. Kirk Sanders, the Chief Technology Officer at Pacific Aerospace, had been chosen as the secretary of Science and Technology. Sam Turnbull, the owner of Penny-wise, the largest supermarket chain in California, was chosen as the secretary of Civil Supplies. He had come to them with a well thought out plan for collecting and distributing food and other essentials using his warehouses and supermarkets, and had placed his entire fleet of trucks, which numbered 500, at their service. Henry Winkerman, the Deputy Commissioner of LAPD, had volunteered as the secretary of Law and Order. Judge Thomas Gayhill, the Chief Justice of the LA County Superior Court, had been appointed the Chief Justice of the State Supreme Court.

Kate's entire office staff consisted of friends, colleagues and secretaries from her architecture firm. She had always been popular at work. In the past few days, her stature had risen to a point where people felt a fierce sense of loyalty and an immense pride in working for her.

General Paterson and Kate had decided that it would be best to let the individual cabinet members appoint their own office staff and plan their functions. Kate would hold daily cabinet meetings to monitor the progress and to suggest changes.

Within a week after setting up her government, Kate had established an administrative routine and come to feel quite self-assured and in control. She had set up her office at her former work place. The familiar location and the familiar faces added to her confidence. She was at work by 7:00 a.m. every morning. 7:00 - 8:00 she would carefully read the report from each secretary. 8:00 - 9:00 she met with her personal assistant to be briefed by him and to give him instructions on issues that needed attention. 9:00 - 11:30 she spent a half-hour with each cabinet Secretary to get updates and to set directions. A working lunch answering calls, reading mail – mail service had been restored - from 11:30 a.m. to 12:30 p.m. Afternoons, from 12:30 p.m. to

5:00 p.m. she spent on the road, inspecting various sites, stopping to talk to people and generally getting a first hand knowledge of the way things were shaping up. She would return to her office at 5:30 p.m. and prepare for her half-hour question and answer session with the public on KLAN which started at 6:30 p.m. She would return to the office at 8:00 p.m. and work until 9:30 p.m. attending to last minute matters. It would be 10:30 by the time she got home. She would go to bed around 11:00, tired but happy. She hardly had any time for Peter, or his girlfriend.

An environment of genuine goodwill and cooperation had developed in The State of Good Hope. The office of relief operations had been successful in restoring almost complete normalcy - normalcy in the day-to-day mechanical sense. Thousands of wounded had been treated. Voluntary mobile units consisting of doctors and nurses made house calls treating the sick and the wounded. Broken water and gas pipes had been fixed. Roads had been cleared of debris and repair work was underway, where needed. The communications network was pretty much fully restored. There were now three TV stations in addition to KLAN, providing round-the-clock service. Telephone service was completely restored, except for homes and businesses connected directly to the damaged switches. Dr. Sanders had arranged for cellular phones to be provided in such cases, so everyone had access to phones. They still couldn't call from anywhere to anywhere, but at least they all had a phone available. Power was a problem. Dr. Sanders had quickly ascertained that they only had about 25 percent of their normal power supply available. However, since most businesses and industries had shut down, 25 percent of the normal power supply met 75 percent of their needs. They needed some amount of cutting back to meet the deficit. He had, therefore, ordered power cuts for four hours everyday, from 9:00 a.m. to 11:00 a.m. and 2:30 p.m. to 4:30 p.m. Their normal supply of gas had not been affected, so that was mercifully not an issue.

Sam Turnbull had done a fantastic job of setting up the distribution network. Actually, it was business as usual except for the financial transactions. The same buyers would acquire different types of goods from various wholesalers and arrange for shipment to warehouses. Warehouse managers, in turn, shipped the goods to various supermarkets as per the inventory managers' requests. Nothing much had changed, except no money changed hands.

Once people began to feel comfortable with the complete absence of money, things began to be done more smoothly and efficiently than before. The supermarket managers had been instructed to ration all items. They had set up fairly liberal rules to prevent hoarding. No more than two gallons of milk per day per family, no more than two pounds of bread, and so on. The first couple of days, there were some ugly scenes with people demanding more of something or other and the store refusing to give it to them. However, when people saw a smooth flow of goods of all kinds they stopped making demands. In the beginning, they had to go through check-out counters where clerks checked to make sure no one got more than their share. Pretty soon there was no need for checks, and check-out counters had been eliminated. It was quite a sight to see people walk in, pick up exactly what they needed, and walk out. No lines of any sort. Even the poorest of neighborhoods had dispensed with check-out counters. Sam had, in fact, taken particular care to keep the supermarkets in the less affluent areas particularly well stocked so as to inspire confidence in the people.

All banks were closed. All malls had been closed as a safety measure. Schools remained closed. Many of the mansions in Beverly Hills and in other affluent areas had been converted to shelters for the homeless. In most cases, the rich had given up their houses and gone to live with friends and relatives. In some cases, they had gone a step further and taken in total strangers and provided food, room and clothing. It was as though Mother Teresa's missionaries had taken over the entire state.

A certain Father Duncan had announced the creation of The Church of Good Hope. He conducted daily service on TV from 8:00 a.m. to 8:30 a.m. He continued Kate's message of sharing and cooperation and spent his 30 minutes on TV trying to convince people that it was their spiritual faith that kept The State of Good Hope floating. The State of Good Hope was now over a thousand miles from California and moving west at the rate of about 120 miles per day.

After a week in office, Kate continued to worry about the slow pace with which the Science Council was progressing. There was no new information from the Science Council. Beyond the theories they had come up with to provide plausible explanations of the phenomenon, they had not produced much else. It was not for lack of trying, they just had no clue. There was near unanimity that movement deep within the earth's crust had created a subterranean gas pipeline which had caused an enormous gas build-up under Southern California. They believed that the gas under enormous pressure had caught fire and the mixture of hot air and gases under pressure had ripped Southern California apart along the San Andreas' fault line. The resulting jet stream of hot air and gases had propelled the landmass at a speed of about 80 miles per hour initially, and thereafter possibly due to further movement in the crust acting like a regulation valve, the jet stream speed had probably reduced leading to a steady speed of around 5 miles per hour. Through a stroke of luck, the mixture of hot air and gases had probably found escape routes from several points at the bottom of the separated landmass creating enough of a vertical force to allow the landmass to float. In short, they believed that nature had created a perfect, gigantic, rocket powered ship which would continue to float and move as long as there was an adequate supply of gas and as long as the horizontal and vertical jet streams had a clear passage. If the slightest crust movement blocked the flow of jet streams, The State of Good Hope could stop moving, or stop floating, or both.

The Science Council had been puzzled by the sinking of tall buildings and heavy aircraft on the separated landmass. Some of them believed that under the pressure of hot air and gases, the prevailing surface pressure distribution on the landmass, at the moment of separation, had played a critical role in determining the thickness of the earth's crust in the breakaway segment. They believed that at the moment of separation a certain kind of dynamic balance had been reached with the thickness in the crust of the breakaway landmass varying in accordance with the surface pressure on the ground. The crust was thicker where there was greater pressure, up to a critical threshold, they reasoned. Beyond the critical threshold, the ground simply caved in and by sheer luck no upward passage for the jet stream had been created. Had an upward passage been created, it would essentially have behaved like a volcano and chances of survival would have been slim. The scientists were not sure how thin the crust would be where the ground pressure had been low. Some felt that the crust at such points could be very thin and any change in pressure distribution on the floating landmass could lead to the ground caving in, and worse, possibly create an upward jet stream causing a volcanic explosion. Others had felt that the crust would be thick enough under the natural pressure distribution coming from the weight of the ground. The debate had continued with no consensus emerging. The only sure way to find out was to perform extensive testing of the surface as well as the bottom of the floating landmass, which clearly was impossible given the circumstances. This had worried Kate. She wanted to know two things above all. Did they have enough gas to keep them floating until they hit another landmass? How sensitive was the crust to changes in surface pressure distribution? She found the answer to the second question the very next day. They would not find the answer to the first question for a while.

Kate heard from Henry Winkerman, the Secretary of Law and Order, the next day, about the KBEE helicopter crash. They had recovered the tape the cameraman had recorded. When Kate saw the tape, she realized that the crust was extremely sensitive to changes in surface pressure distribution. There were not more than a 100 people surrounding the helicopter when the whole area caved in. That was 100 people plus a helicopter in a 100 feet by 50 feet parcel of land. Many crowded malls would probably have greater pressure. She immediately decided that all malls and schools would remain closed. She issued an ordinance prohibiting more than 50 people from gathering at any one place, including churches, libraries, any public building. She instructed all TV stations to play the KBEE tape several times along with a message about how too many people gathering in one spot could cause the ground to cave in. She had the tape shipped to the Science Council and requested President Walters to issue an order prohibiting any American or foreign TV crew from landing on The State of Good Hope. It was much too dangerous.

CHAPTER 11

P resident Walters had been growing more and more impatient with the Science Council. It was now 25 days since The State of Good Hope had broken away. All these days they had been hoping that The State of Good Hope would collide gently with one of the Hawaiian islands and come to rest peacefully. Two days ago he had received word that The State of Good Hope had sailed just north of the Hawaiian islands, missing Oahu by about 200 miles and Kauai by a mere 100 miles or so. That was practically a hair's breadth compared to the vastness of the Pacific. President Walters had called Kate to console her. Kate and her cabinet had been waiting with bated breath for the past three weeks, ever since NASA had predicted that if The State of Good Hope held its course, it would collide with either Oahu or Kauai. As it had turned out, The State of Good Hope had held its course for most of three weeks, but had unaccountably veered northward and just missed both Oahu and Kauai.

The scientists at the Science Council had thought it could either be a change in the Pacific current or a slight change in the direction of the jet stream propelling The State of Good Hope that had caused the last minute deviation. Father Duncan, the founder of The Church of Good Hope, had felt differently about the last minute change in course. He had increased his daily service to an hour and had preached that God willed them to be his messengers a while longer so that the world may watch them live in peace and harmony amidst the tribulations that had befallen them.

"We are God's messengers, carrying the message of peace and love. He wants us to go around the world so that others may observe and learn that our lives are not defined by the material things around us, but by the spiritual force within us. The same spiritual force that makes this great state float and move," he preached.

To Kate, Father Duncan's interpretation had made at least as much sense as the theories offered by the Science Council. If anything, this further increased the faith of the people of The State of Good Hope. The spirit of sharing, cooperation and working together increased to new levels. They had achieved a state of communal harmony unheard of in recorded history.

Back in Washington D.C., however, things were far from harmonious. President Walters had called his Secretary of State, Secretary of Defense and the Director of CIA for a special meeting. James Cornby, the Secretary of State, Arthur Hill, the Secretary of Defense, and Jack Kent, the Director of CIA had all assembled in haste. They were all seasoned men. Men President Walters counted on during moments of crises. Like the present one.

"Gentlemen," President Walters began, "you know why you are here. The State of Good Hope has missed Hawaii and is now headed for Southern China. If it holds its course, that is. Jack Kent here has expressed to me his concerns about the security threat this exposes us to. I want us to assess the security situation and recommend a course of action."

The reason for the concern was obvious. The State of Good Hope had among the most advanced fighter aircraft and missile systems in the world. It not only had a stockpile of these, it had manufacturing facilities equipped with highly sophisticated machinery and enough raw materials to produce hundreds more. In fact, it would not have been an exaggeration to say that next to the mainland U.S.. The State of Good Hope had the most advanced defense capability in the world. If these fell into the wrong hands, U.S. military supremacy would be seriously compromised. And there were no hands less suited to receive these advanced defense equipment, than those of the Chinese. With vastly inferior nuclear and missile technology, the Chinese had still managed to dictate terms to the U.S. all through the eighties and nineties. They had drawn the Americans in slowly and deliberately. The Americans had first approached China in the post-Mao era hoping to influence them economically first and then politically, to push them away from communism towards democracy. But driven by the capitalist forces that fuel the American economy, the trickle of economic activity in China had grown in size to an extent where practically all the U.S manufacturing facilities from Hong Kong, Singapore and Taiwan had relocated to mainland China. In less than 10 years, the tables had been turned on the Americans to a point where the U.S. Government had been forced to look the other way during the Tiananmen Square massacre in 1989. The American industries now needed China for its vast consumer base and cheap manufacturing facilities, more than China needed American technology and money. The nineties had continued in this vein with China dictating economic terms to the U.S. and doing what was politically expedient to further the cause of the communist party brass. Towards the end of the nineties, China had made enormous economic strides and stood poised to emerge as the only challenger to the U.S superpower status. In this delicate situation, the acquisition by China of the defense capabilities on The State of Good Hope would have virtually guaranteed superpower status to China. This would completely change the political and economic equation between China and the U.S. and would have inevitable global repercussions. The economic boom in the U.S. and most of Europe would collapse overnight. The consequences would be terrible. The people gathered at President Walters' meeting were acutely aware of all this. The question was, what preventive measures could they take? What options did they have?

"What's the likelihood of The State of Good Hope colliding with China?" asked James Cornby. The question was addressed to Jack Kent, the Director of CIA.

"Hard to say. Just because of its sheer size, the probability of a collision with China is pretty high. NASA says it is too early to tell. It may drift north and head toward Japan, or head south towards Australia, or go somewhere in between towards Philippines and Indonesia. Who knows," Kent said.

"Australia would be the most optimistic scenario," President Walters commented.

"Don't be so sure Mr. President," the director said, "there is no saying what impact this kind of a gold mine has on a nation. Any nation. I wouldn't be the least bit surprised if Australia starts acting like a big power, pressing for a seat on the UN security council, expanding G7 to G8, who knows. Give people strong teeth and they want to chew on your bones." The rest of them nodded.

"For the time being, we must assume the worst case scenario. Suppose The State of Good Hope collides with

China. Are we prepared to accept that?" asked the Secretary of Defense.

"Impossible! The American people cannot allow that," President Walters said.

"What news from the Science Council? How long do they think The State of Good Hope can keep floating?" asked James Cornby, his tone of voice suggesting that the problem would be solved if The State of Good Hope stopped floating.

"Jim! I hope you didn't mean that!" the President said angrily. He was known to be an emotional man.

"No. No. Mr. President, please! I meant nothing of the sort," Cornby hastened to add, "just wondering what they thought the chances were."

"Then let's stop wondering," President Walters said. "Let's make two assumptions. That The State of Good Hope will continue to float as long as necessary. And that we all fervently hope and pray for the safety of Kate and her people," he looked pointedly at the Secretary of State.

"Well, then, we are back to our problem, aren't we?" the CIA director asked, not much impressed by the President's display of emotions. He had seen many of them come and go.

"Yes, we are, and that's what you are here for. To recommend a solution." President Walters snapped.

Arthur Hill, the Secretary of Defense, stepped in sensing rising tension. "Any chance we can pressurize China into not interfering?"

"Are you kidding? Remember Tiananmen Square? We can't even pressurize them into outlawing software piracy and you think we can prevent them from grabbing the most sophisticated defense equipment on earth? Not a chance! What are you going to do? Threaten them with nukes, ICBMs? They've got them too. Ours maybe better. But they have them too. There is no preemptive strike in this game. Especially if they sit still until after the collision with Good Hope, and then move in. We can't possibly endanger the lives of 12 million of our own citizens with a first strike. They couldn't have asked for better security. They've got us where they want, they know it. I bet the commie bastards are drooling over it even now." Jack Kent was being very forthright. Those who knew him well knew that could possibly mean only one thing. He had something up his sleeve. A shrewd mix of disarming honesty and alarming dishonesty was the secret to his success.

"Yes, I agree. Once it hits China, nothing can stop a Chinese takeover. I wish the Science Council came up with a way of slowing it down. Or change its course toward Australia or even Antarctica. But they don't have a clue what the damn thing is about. I feel so emasculated, like I'm watching a bunch of thugs ransacking my home right in front of me..." President Walters was interrupted by Kent.

"Mr. President, I have a suggestion." They all sat up, attentive. Kent continued, "what if we selectively disable the most sensitive equipment?"

"How would we do that?" responded Arthur Hill. "There are hundreds of aircraft, thousands of missiles. Several manufacturing facilities. Thousands of sensitive design documents, spare parts,...can't be done."

"Unless we get the Governor to cooperate," Kent said. He was referring to Kate.

"Cooperate how?" the President asked.

"By voluntarily destroying all sensitive material including equipment, spare parts, documents, everything," Kent said.

"Look, we haven't been able to give them an iota of help. The poor souls are lost in the ocean. They must be scared beyond reason. I am amazed they haven't panicked into some sort of mass hysteria. I attribute that to Kate's charisma and ability to instill hope in the people. How can I ask her to go about destroying stuff, for the well being of people thousands of miles away? If I ask her that, she'll know we don't care any more. They'll think we have given up on them. They are Americans too, for God's sake! How is our security different from their security?" The President was getting emotional again.

"The plain and simple truth, Mr. President, is that it is. Our security is fundamentally different from theirs. They are drifting uncontrollably into unwelcome areas. We are here, safe in our haven. They have some of our most prized possessions. If someone else gets hold of them, our haven will be less safe." More plain speaking from Kent.

"Mr. President, Jack's suggestion has merit. There is no harm in trying. If she doesn't agree, we'll think of something else," James Cornby came out in support of the CIA Director's proposal.

"We can't do this to people clutching at straws. We cannot in good conscience ask them to do this," the

President looked at the Defense Secretary expecting support. But none was forthcoming.

President Walters was not a man given to indecision or vacillations. He was a firm man, but he was also a man with a heart. He believed passionately in everything that America stood for. He shared the anguish and despair of Kate and her people, perhaps more acutely than anyone else on the mainland. After disaster struck Southern California, he had tossed about many a night angry and frustrated that their evacuation plans had failed and that he could do nothing to ensure the safety of 12 million of his citizens. The plan that Kent had just proposed was completely unacceptable to him. He found it abhorrent. There had to be another way, though he couldn't think of one.

Another option would, in fact, soon emerge. Though, had anyone suggested it as an option to President Walters at that moment, he would have rejected it with even greater vehemence.

CHAPTER 12

*W*hen Kate got a call from President Walters the next morning, she was stunned. The President had told her of the security concerns and the plan Jack Kent had in mind.

"I am not endorsing Jack's plan Kate, but I want you to think about it. I would like to squash it right here and now. But I don't have any alternatives. The security concerns are real. All too real. If someone leaks the situation to the media, there will be complete chaos. All kinds of extremist factions will emerge advocating ridiculous options like bombing China, bombing you, anything," President Walters stopped. What the President had been saying had barely registered on Kate's shocked brain.

"But...but, Mr. President," she stuttered, "this plan, it is impossible. Just imagine, if we go about destroying all the defense facilities and the people got wind of it. It will collapse, the whole government structure will collapse. What we have created here, these past four weeks, is a system of faith and cooperation, Mr. President. If we do anything in the slightest degree to shake the people's trust, the whole thing will fall apart. We really have no checks and balances other than the strong bond and the selfless sharing this disaster has inspired in us. It is a new experience to all of us, giving up our individual needs for the common good. But we have adapted remarkably well to embrace the new lifestyle. You have to see it to believe it. The millionaires opening their doors to the starving homeless, the Hispanic gangs helping in construction sites, it is absolutely incredible." She had recovered her wits sufficiently now.

"I know Kate, I know. I've seen it on TV. You and your people have emerged as a beacon of hope for humanity. You are making us search our souls in a way that American people have never done before. This is bigger than the revolutionary wars, bigger than the civil war, bigger than the civil rights movements. In fact, it is bigger than America. It is a lesson for the whole world. I do listen regularly to Father Duncan, you know, and I tend to agree with him. But the instincts for self preservation are quite strong too. It is a fundamental human dichotomy, self preservation at any cost versus an infinite capacity to share and care. Hitler versus Mother Teresa. Mahatma Gandhi versus the British empire. Jack Kent versus Kate Upshaw."

Kate was surprised for the second time in ten minutes. She was not aware of the passions and emotions that stirred the President from within.

"Thank you, Mr. President," she said, "it is not that we are special. It is just the circumstances we are in. But Jack Kent's plan is impractical. It can't be done. There are two problems. First, how do we go about destroying all the stuff? I am not sure exactly what we are talking about here, I'll have to check with Frank Jewell, my Defense Secretary. I would imagine this would involve destroying fighter aircraft, missiles, perhaps nuclear bombs. What would we do with them? Can't dump them in the ocean, we can't even go near the ocean. Could have blown up the planes and missiles and detonated the explosives, but it is too dangerous. The crust on this landmass is very fragile. The

Science Council folks haven't come out with their opinion on it yet, but from what I've seen, it is like an egg shell. The slightest increase in pressure, and it'll crack. We've been lucky so far. The hot gases haven't found their way up. But if they do, this whole place could become a blazing volcano. The second problem is even worse than the first. I could somehow figure out the logistics of destruction. A few of us can carry the damn missiles and throw them over the edge, if it comes to that. But if the news spreads, and it is inevitable, I am damn sure it will, it will have a demoralizing effect on the people. It will be the 'me first' culture all over again. And it will return with a vengeance. This whole fragile edifice, quite literally built on faith and hope, will collapse like nine pins. We won't recover from that Mr. President, I guarantee you, we won't. We won't make it to China, or anywhere much further than wherever we are right now." Her voice broke.

President Walters was sobbing openly now. He had been teary-eyed for a while, but this was more than he could bear. He had broken into muffled sobs. For a while all the two of them could hear was each other crying, trying to suppress their sobs. President Walters recovered first.

"Give some thought to it Kate," he said, "if you come up with any viable plan at all, I'll support it. No matter what. I am prepared to risk my presidency over this issue. But remember, this is bigger than me. Once the situation becomes public and people's passions are aroused, it will go out of control. We've got to act fast and in strict secrecy. I'll be thinking hard too. But I am not getting much help here, most people here are in the self preservation mode. I am counting on you and your people to come up with something in the next couple of days."

Kate was moved to tears again. "Thank you Mr. President," she said, "I hope I get a chance to meet you and to express my gratitude in person. Thank you."

"You will, Kate, you will," President Walters said. The call had lasted thirty minutes, but it had forged the bond of a lifetime.

CHAPTER 13

*K*ate canceled all her appointments for the rest of the day. She called an emergency meeting of her cabinet for 2:00 p.m. The rest of the morning she spent in her office, weighing her options. There were none. They were caught in a situation the old adage described as a choice between the devil and the deep sea. Except they had one less option. It was just the deep sea for them.

The cabinet assembled at 2:00 p.m. in Kate's office. They were all there. Frank Jewell, the Defense Secretary, Gail warland, the Secretary of Relief Operations, Dr. Sanders, the Secretary of Science and Technology, Sam Turnbull, the Secretary of Civil Supplies, and Henry Winkerman, the Secretary of Law and Order. She had asked General Paterson to attend as well. When they saw General Paterson, the cabinet members knew this was not a regular cabinet meeting. There was something special brewing.

Kate swore them to strict secrecy and then told them about the call from President Walters. Seasoned as they were by now in dealing with extraordinary events, they still went through the predictable reactions. Absurd. How could they? If they couldn't help, they should at least leave them alone to grapple with fate. And so on. General Paterson's reaction was the most subdued, and even he voiced strong protest. Kate listened patiently. She knew what they were going through. She was still going through the same reactions inside, though she maintained her composure externally. It was too much for Gail Warland to see Kate sitting impassively, listening to them.

"How can you just sit there Kate? Tell us what you think," she said. There was an edge in her voice.

"Gail," said Kate calmly, "these are exactly my thoughts. If you don't see me beating my chest and flailing my arms about, it's because I've had six hours to do that. It's an impasse. No solution. And don't think I am all calm and unperturbed. I am like this freaky phenomenon. All hot and pressured inside, but nothing on the outside. I don't know how much longer I can take it."

This was the closest to an outburst they had seen from Kate. General Paterson walked over to her, pressed her shoulders softly, and said, "Don't let this get to you Kate. We need you. You will see us through, we are confident of that."

Everyone nodded in agreement. The meeting broke up at 6:00 p.m. amidst expressions of solidarity and support. They would mull over the situation and reassemble at 8:00 a.m. the next day.

Kate declined General Paterson's invitation for dinner. She preferred to be alone. She sat in her office for another half-hour going over the afternoon's discussions in her mind. Finally she gave up and decided to go home.

On the way home, she turned the car radio on, more to give her fevered mind a break than anything else. Father Duncan's familiar voice came on. He now had an evening service on the radio, in addition to his morning service on TV. Father Duncan was quoting from the Bible to describe how God tests the spiritual character of man by inserting seemingly insurmountable obstacles in his path. "The outer-eye sees the obstacles, and the senses react. The brain and the body panic. But the inner-eye must see God hiding behind every obstacle, waiting for us to cross the hurdle so He can reveal Himself," he was saying.

Kate felt inspired. Why not consult Father Duncan? He would bring a fresh perspective. Their deliberations had led nowhere. Maybe Father Duncan could help. She turned the car in the direction of The Church of Good Hope. Father Duncan lived in a small cottage behind the church building. The caretaker told Kate to wait in Father Duncan's office. He would return at 8:00 p.m.

It was a little past eight when Father Duncan returned. He knew Kate. Kate had, of course, seen him on TV, but he appeared more frail in person. His inner calm shone through even more forcefully than on TV. He wouldn't hear of discussing anything with Kate until after dinner. Kate shared his frugal meal, made the richer by the gracious host. She found him witty, well informed, and charming. He even managed to get her mind off the oppressive details that had been chewing on her innards the whole day.

After dinner Father Duncan took Kate into his office and closed the door. "What is it Kate? Tell me, my child. Lord knows you have plenty on your mind. What's bothering you?"

The warmth and directness of his tone surprised and reassured Kate. Within a few minutes she summarized the day's events, starting with President Walters' call and ending with the sense of frustration and helplessness she and her cabinet felt.

Father Duncan did not speak for a while. He just sat with his chin resting on his right palm. Finally, he said, "This doesn't surprise me, Kate. We are now far, far, away from the rest of America. We maybe just 3000 miles away physically, but spiritually, we're light-years away. If, by some miracle, planes could land on The State of Good Hope tomorrow, we could all be back in America the same day. For most of us, just our corporeal selves will be thrust back in the midst of mainstream America. Spiritually, we are different. Not just from America, from the whole world. This divine experience, I prefer to call it divine, has rekindled in us something that civilization left behind in the primeval forests thousands of years ago. Humanity, compassion, feeling the presence of God. That's what I see here. What takes years of hardship and deprivation for ordinary priests and monks to achieve, the people of Good Hope have achieved in a matter of four weeks amidst this chaos and uncertainty. They've achieved this by doing what no one else has done before on this scale. Opening their hearts to others. It's a simple concept every religion preaches. But here we are seeing it in practice. Perhaps this is how it was, thousands of years ago, before the material world masked the spiritual world. God has given us a chance to awaken our spirituality. We cannot return to our old lives."

Kate had been listening, fascinated. It was not clear to her what the Father had meant. "Yes, Father, I can understand that. But what are we to do? How do we deal with this situation?" she asked.

"Break free, Kate. Break free. We have nothing in common with America anymore, physically, or spiritually. They cannot help us. We have to help ourselves."

"Father, do you mean...?"

Father Duncan nodded.

"Yes, but how?"

"President Walters has offered you help. Call him and discuss the idea, he will help you."

"What about the people here? How will they react to formally severing all links with America?"

"You deal with the rest of the world. You convince them. I'll convince the people of Good Hope." Father Duncan was a practical man too.

CHAPTER 14

*K*ate didn't sleep at all that night. The day's events had been too much for her. First the bad news from President Walters, and then the startlingly simple solution proposed by Father Duncan. Could they pull it off? How would they go about it anyway? How do you create a new country? This was beyond her realm of political experience. She would have to consult with her cabinet and, if they approved, discuss it with President Walters. He would probably kill the idea right away. She could not imagine him doing anything else. And that would be that. Back to square one. What next? She had no answers. She would have to take it one step at a time.

But Father Duncan had been right. Things fell into place so smoothly and events occurred so fast that even as Kate wondered what to do and how to do it, The Nation of Good Hope was born.

Kate's cabinet had embraced Father Duncan's plan with an enthusiasm that had startled her. They all thought it was a master stroke, the only logical alternative. Made perfect sense. If the U.S. couldn't help them, was, rather, intent on destroying them, then why call themselves Americans? They just had to figure out the details. Kate had to call President Walters and seek his help. If he chose not to help, they would worry about how to put pressure on him and the international community. They had to let them do it. What could they do to stop them anyway? No one could approach them by sea or air. Certainly not in large numbers. And they had a strong enough military to ward off most countries. No one would dare attack them, General Paterson had said. The cabinet decided that Kate would call President Walters right away and General Paterson would, in the meantime, put the military on alert.

When Kate called President Walters with Father Duncan's proposal, he had been shocked. The possibility of a separate country had not even entered his head. His first reaction was one of rage and blind opposition. But Kate had persisted. She had presented the arguments Father Duncan had made, cogently, without getting emotional. Soon President Walters had seen the beautiful simplicity of the plan. It would give him a way of dealing with the domestic pressure. It was clear that Good Hope had to defend itself against who ever maybe tempted by the bag of goodies. China, Australia, whatever. If they did it as Americans, then America would get embroiled in a global row of unprecedented proportions. Even a third world war was possible. But if they defended themselves as The Nation of Good Hope, a separate and sovereign country, then who could blame them?

America could of course support them, if they chose to, like they would their NATO allies. It was a remarkably simple plan. They would just play up the safety of 12 million Americans and their right to defend themselves against foreign aggressors to garner domestic support. A few well placed leaks to the national dailies would take care of that. But internationally, the first move would have to come from Kate. Or at least appear to. Kate could go on TV, live, and address the global community to explain what she was doing and her reasons. She would have to formally request the UN Secretary General to intervene on her behalf in her discussions, for independence, with the

U.S. Government. The U.S. would make a show of protest, kick their heels and scream a bit. Finally, good sense would prevail. There would, of course, be some saber-rattling on the part of China, Russia, maybe Australia, and even India. But with global support backing Kate, they would have to shut up.

In the next few weeks, President Walters proved what a consummate politician he was. Not even his wife knew, or suspected, that he was in on the whole deal.

First some articles appearing in The New York Times, Washington Post and The Los Angeles Times, had suggested that Kate Upshaw would soon ask for sovereign status. The pros and cons surrounding the issue had been presented and an environment of genuine debate had been created among the intelligentsia. Using this as a pretext, President Walters had met with the Senate and Congressional committees, and with his own cabinet members, the chiefs of staff of the Army, Air Force and Navy, and Jack Kent, the CIA director, to impartially assess the situation.

Kate's global address on CNN had been timed perfectly, to strike at the precise moment of indecision to tilt the balance. Kate had been fantastic. She had surpassed her previous performance. The rough edges from her previous speech were gone. She had made the world cry with her and cheer for her.

Following Kate's address came her telephone request to the UN Secretary General asking for intervention and assistance in their efforts to secede from America. Amidst protests and threats, numerous meetings of the UN security Council, the G7, the G5, ASEAN, pretty much every conceivable international body, The nation of Good Hope had been ratified as a sovereign country. The

U.S. had insisted on a special defense treaty giving the U.S. the right to wage war against any country threatening The Nation of Good Hope. July 6th 1998 became the official independence day of The Nation of Good Hope. Governor Kate became President Kate. They decided that they would formally adopt the U.S. constitution as their own in the future, if and when they settled down to a stable existence. In the meantime, Kate and her cabinet would run the contry guided by the spirit of the U.S. constitution.

Nothing much else changed on The Nation of Good Hope. They had now been drifting for 65 days and were some 6800 miles southwest of California, heading straight for southern China.

Quite remarkably, President Walters had emerged stronger politically than ever. His approval rating had risen to over 90 percent. He had shown his patriotism by fervently arguing against giving sovereign status to Good Hope in the beginning. Had given in under pressure from the UN and when cogent arguments about the need for Good Hope to defend itself without compromising American political and economic interests, were presented to him. The public sentiments had been with him on both occasions. He was now the second most popular head of state in the world, behind Kate.

No one ever heard about the discreet calls President Walters had made to the U.S. ambassador to the UN, a career diplomat personally appointed to the position by him.

CHAPTER 15

*K*ate had been in office as president almost five months now. They had traveled nearly 18000 miles. For a long time their course had held steady. Straight towards Southern China and Taiwan. When they were about a thousand miles away, just as they entered the Philippine Sea, quite inexplicably they changed direction and started moving towards the Philippines. No one knew why. Father Duncan had an explanation. God was not yet welcome on Chinese shores and, hence, the divine ship had steered clear, according to him.

By divine ordinance, or sheer chance, The Nation of Good Hope had sailed past the Philippines and Malaysia, dexterously weaved in and out of the myriad Indonesian isles that dotted the Indian Ocean and continued on a southwesterly course towards Antarctica. This had caused a great deal of concern among Kate and her cabinet. The Nation of Good Hope was not ready for the Antarctic cold. If their course held, they would enter frigidly cold waters in another month. Frantic preparations were launched to get ready for the cold climate. Overnight, quilt clubs and knitting clubs mushroomed by the thousands. People began boarding up windows. Kate and Dr. Sanders, the Secretary of Science and Technology, were thinking seriously of alternatives for mass producing insulation material to keep houses warm. About then, things changed for the better.

Just north of the Tropic of Capricorn, The Nation of Good Hope changed course again. Ever so slowly, it started

moving northwest until it made a ninety-degree turn and
headed towards India. They were in warm waters again and
the cold weather preparations ceased. If their course held,
they could expect to collide with India or Sri Lanka in a
little less than a month.

Father Duncan again attributed the change in direction
to providence. "Spiritual India beckons us," he said to his
followers who now numbered more than 6 million, "prepare
for a landing, we have work to do there. They need us." He
went on to describe the work of Mother Teresa, how she had
worked for the upliftment of the poor and the dispossessed.
Mother Teresa had passed away just a few months earlier.
He linked their change in course to Mother Teresa's death.
"The torch has been passed. It is now in our hands. Accept
it with faith and the Lord will see us home," he said.

Even for his faithful followers, accepting poor, third-
world, India, as home was hard. No matter its past spiritual
glory, the pictures of poverty stricken, dirty, bedraggled
India, so popular in the western media, were frozen in their
minds.

"From southern China to southern India, not much has
changed. We are doomed to be part of some third-world
country," a TV show host had lamented.

As The Nation of Good Hope approached India,
there was growing concern among its citizens. They were
now less than 300 miles away from the tip of the Indian
peninsula. Kate and her cabinet were concerned too. They
did not particularly relish the enforced proximity with
India. But it was probably not too bad, wasn't Southern
California adjoining poor Mexico? Some argued that, that
was different. It had not mattered. The vastness of the U.S.
had dwarfed the Mexican influence. The story here would

be different. There was no way they could remain isolated from gigantic India. A mere 12 million of them would be insignificant in number compared to the one billion Indians. They had no choice, in any case. The thought uppermost in their minds was the safety of their citizens. How would India react?

The India of yore, under the influence of Gandhi and Nehru, had been a peace loving country. But under provocation from its neighbors, Pakistan and China, a more belligerent and fundamentalist India had emerged in the recent past. Just a couple of months earlier, India had caught the whole world by surprise and exploded several nuclear bombs. The ensuing U.S. sanctions and the sanctions from Europe and Japan, made under American pressure, had created a bitter feeling towards America amongst most Indians. They had felt justifiably betrayed by the double standards the U.S. foreign policy makers adopted in offering economic assistance to oppressive China while ignoring, even punishing, democratic India. What effect would all this have on The Nation of Good Hope, if, and when, it collided with India?

Kate had called President Walters for advice.

"Don't worry Kate," President Walters had said, "Don't believe everything you read in the press. India is a fundamentally democratic country, like the United States. They won't do anything rash. I'll have the seventh fleet moved closer to India, just in case. Remember, you'll be there for just a few days. Separate country or not, you are all welcome in the United States. You just have to request it and we'll have you out of there in no time."

This had reassured Kate.

When they were 300 miles from the Indian tip, they learnt from NASA that their speed had fallen to around 4 miles per hour. "Nothing to worry about, probably just crust movement altering the jet stream velocity. We'll keep a close watch on it," they had said to Dr. Sanders who had called to enquire. Dr. Sanders was not satisfied. If the velocity of the horizontal jet stream had changed, then so could the velocity of the vertical jet stream. While the former would merely slow them down, an appreciable reduction in the latter could cause them to sink. Dr. Sanders ordered aerial surveys to monitor the jet stream velocity. They could not measure the jet stream velocity from the air, but the infrared detectors showed a strong jet stream and a strong water current, just like before.

The molten rock continued to pour out in large quantities from the side that had been the Southern California coast. Again, they could not monitor accurately enough to determine if the volume of molten rock pouring out had changed. The water temperature was almost the same as it was when it had last been measured during the sea-evacuation attempt.

"At least there is no obvious change in the jet stream activity," Dr. Sanders thought, "which means there is still plenty of gas left to push us another 300 miles." He ordered aerial surveys to be conducted every two hours and the results to be sent directly to him.

The next morning Dr. Sanders got another call from NASA. Their speed had fallen alarmingly. They were now moving at a little over 3 miles per hour. They were still 200 miles away from the Indian shore. Could they make it? The aerial surveys showed no measurable drop in jet stream activity or in the molten rock flow. This was not comforting to Dr. Sanders. He knew there had to be a difference in the horizontal jet stream flow because NASA had reported that their speed had fallen and their speed was directly proportional to that of the horizontal jet stream. If their speed, as measured by NASA, had reduced, then the speed of the jet stream would have reduced by the same ratio. It was just that the sensors used in the aerial survey simply did not have the resolution needed to measure the difference. They had not been built for that purpose. There was nothing he could do. What could he do even if knew The Nation of Good Hope was going to stop moving and sink the next day because it ran out of gas? Nothing. There was nothing they could do to move 12 million people to safety in a day. Not even in a month. No country in the region had that kind of resources.

He discussed the situation with Kate and they debated their options. Kate could call the Prime Minister of India, or President Walters, or both. But what good would that do? The Indian Government had already begun monitoring them. They had seen several Indian Air Force planes flying near by. General Paterson had learnt from the U.S. Army contacts he had continued to maintain that an Indian aircraft carrier was hovering in the vicinity. Kate decided that even though the Indian Government couldn't help them if they needed evacuation, it would be a good idea to call the Indian Prime Minister and chat with him. After all, it was the American custom to call first before dropping in on your neighbor. And if their luck held, they would be dropping in on their neighbor in less than three days.

She checked with President Walters first. He had already been in touch with Akash Dalal, the Indian Prime Minister. The Prime Minister had assured President Walters of full cooperation. The Indian Air Force and

Navy would be constantly monitoring the progress of The Nation of Good Hope. They would be equipped with emergency medical supplies. Army units had already been deployed all over the southern coast of India to assist The Nation of Good Hope after the collision. All coastal areas were going to be evacuated. In fact, they expected large masses of people to flee their homes from the villages, towns and cities even as far away as two hundred miles from the coast. Especially in the southern tip of the Indian Peninsula where they were expected to land if they held their course.

"Prime Minister Dalal is a reasonable man," President Walters told Kate, "he has assured us complete and non-intrusive cooperation. We are monitoring the situation very closely. We have several satellites tracking the region. Aircraft from the seventh fleet can reach the tip of the Indian peninsula in fifteen minutes. We are that close. Knowing we are hanging around nearby will encourage them to behave. Moreover they are quite keen on making amends after the nuclear mess they created," he was referring to the nuclear bombs India had recently exploded.

After that Kate called Prime Minister Dalal. He spoke as though he had been expecting her call.

"Ah, President Upshaw, so good of you to call," he said, "terrible, terrible, this situation. I wish we could have gotten acquainted under better circumstances. Cannot always choose what we do. I will personally ensure full cooperation. We will provide whatever assistance you request. But only at your request. We will not enter your territory, unless invited. We will fully respect your border rights, even under these peculiar circumstances. So, please, do not hesitate. Call us, if you need help."

Kate was reasonably satisfied that he meant what he said. She thanked him for his generosity and his concern and told him that she would avail of his offer if they needed help. At least, it looked like India wouldn't bother them if they collided. The question was, would they collide? Would they make it that far?

Their speed had been falling alarmingly. It seemed to be touch and go. At their current speed of about 3 miles per hour they would need to stay afloat for another three days. Dr. Sanders had told her that if the speed of the horizontal jet stream had reduced it was highly likely that the speed of the vertical jet stream would have reduced too and at some point they may begin to sink. Perhaps even now they were beginning to sink. Who knew? If that happened it would be a terrible shame, to go with a whimper after all that they had endured.

There was also the question of the collision itself. The Science Council had told them that they should expect massive structural collapse as they approached another landmass. They had told them that the extent of the damage would depend on how much frictional contact they would have with the ocean floor. A secondary factor would be their speed at the time of running aground. Again all guesses, they weren't really sure. The one positive news they had received from the Science Council was that they had taken extensive measurements of the ocean floor depth off southern India and compared that against the newly created ocean floor off the Southern California coast. They had found a rough match. Of course it all depended on exactly where they would impinge, but even the approximate match they had found was utterly amazing. There was a chance, just a small chance, that they may not suffer severe structural damage when they ran into India.

Kate had been told by the Science Council that they would have to evacuate the coastal areas, get all people to take shelter in basements and emergency shelters. Fires would most likely break out. It would probably be like a fairly strong earthquake, in the most optimistic scenario. All theories. No one knew for sure. She didn't find the theories comforting. She would go consult with Father Duncan in the evening.

CHAPTER 16

*T*he excitement in India had been building up ever since
The Nation of Good Hope changed course and headed
toward India. Now that it was just 200 miles away, the
excitement had reached fever pitch. Political parties were
already squabbling over how the spoils would be shared.
The southern state of Tamilnadu, where most likely The
Nation of Good Hope would impinge, had laid claim to the
new territory. The other southern states and the northern
states had objected vociferously. It didn't matter that The
Nation of Good Hope was a veritable volcano, they didn't
want the riches of Southern California going just to one
state.

The usual political chaos which passed for a democracy
had grown worse. Far worse. The coalition Government
at the center made up of a ragtag bunch of self-serving
politicians had almost come apart over the subject of how
The Nation of Good Hope was going to be accommodated.
Veiled threats from the U.S. and the firm stand that Prime
Minister Dalal had taken, had forced them to lie low for a
while. All parties had come to an informal agreement that
they would let the dust settle and then they would broach
the subject of what to do with The Nation of Good Hope.
Publicly they all maintained that The Nation of Good Hope
was a sovereign country suffering from a severe calamity
and, hence, its citizens should be treated with the greatest
sympathy. But privately, and in internal party meetings,
they were plotting to take control of The Nation of Good

Hope. They had all tacitly assumed that the Americans - they still referred to the Good Hopers as Americans - would leave sooner or later. To them, it was unthinkable that 12 million Americans would forever settle down at the footsteps of India. Any political party that gained control of The Nation of Good Hope, after the Americans left, would reign supreme for a long time to come.

Some political parties based in the north had even come up with outrageous plans to send millions of people from their constituencies over to The Nation of Good Hope to occupy the region as soon as the Americans left. Given half a chance, each political party, and there were over ten major ones, would have flooded Tamilnadu with people from their constituencies to rush to The Nation of Good Hope, at the right time, to lay claim to whatever land, buildings, equipment, they could. But, under pressure from the U.S., and out of the basic decency that was inherent in him, Prime Minister Dalal had deployed Army troops all along the border with strict orders not to allow anyone within 50 miles of the coast all around the southern peninsula. Any transgressors were to be arrested. In fact, orders had been issued to evacuate everyone who lived within that 50 mile swath of land. Prime Minister Dalal had also placed a ban on groups of people larger than five entering the state of Tamilnadu, unless they were residents of the state, in order to prevent political parties from moving people from other states into Tamilnadu in anticipation of the Southern California gold rush that would surely follow once the Americans left. This had created a great deal of inconvenience and resentment, but the general public had supported the move.

Fortunately, the coastal area in this part of India had no big cities, and, consequently, the population density was not as high as it was further inland. Still, the 400 mile by 50 mile stretch of land was home to some 8 million people who had to be evacuated to make room for their alien brethren. Normally, this would have been a next to impossible task. Indians, especially the villagers, usually resisted evacuation at all costs because of the traditional belief that to abandon your home and land was a sin. Every year the cyclones that ravaged the southeast coast killed thousands of people despite early warnings and evacuation attempts, because of this superstition. But this time, a rumor had taken hold that when The nation of Good Hope arrived it would bring with it massive floods, fire and earthquakes killing all within some unstipulated range. Rumor further had it that the disaster that had struck The Nation of Good Hope was itself a manifestation of the wrath of Goddess Kali and anyone who sighted that unholy land would also incur the Goddess's wrath. This had been sufficient to trigger a mass evacuation on a scale not seen in India since the days of the partition.

People had grabbed what they could of their meager belongings and headed inland using whatever means of transportation they had access to. Though Prime Minister Dalal's orders had called for the evacuation of a 50 mile wide stretch of land, in some parts even people living as far away as two hundred miles from the sea had fled.

Within a span of 15 hours after the rumor took hold, some 10 million people spread over a 35000 square mile area had moved inland and sought shelter in the homes of friends, relatives and acquaintances, public buildings, under trees, along river banks, basically wherever they could. The normal hustle and bustle of everyday life had come to a stand still in the coastal towns and villages. Only the very old, the very ill, and the very foolhardy who paid no heed to Goddess Kali or Prime Minister Dalal, had remained.

Southern India had escaped the agonies of partition 50 years earlier during the Indian independence. It was ironic that a forced union had pretty much the same impact as had a forced division. Only the hatred and violence were missing. The fear of the unknown was very much in evidence.

CHAPTER 17

*K*ate spent the day in anguish and uncertainty. Dr. Sanders had kept her updated with the results of the aerial survey. It was small comfort that the jet stream activity and the molten rock flow had continued undiminished as far as they could tell. However, the latest reports from NASA that reached Dr. Sanders around 5:00 p.m. had warned them that the situation was grave. Their speed had fallen to a little over 2 miles per hour. They had only covered 30 miles in the last 12 hours. The tip of the Indian peninsula was still 170 miles away. At their present speed it would take them another 4 days. The suspense and the agony were unbearable. Should she share the news with the people? How would they react? Would they despair? Or would the faith that Father Duncan had instilled and sustained over a period of 5 months, endure? She couldn't make up her mind. She would seek Father Duncan's advice.

Kate came to visit Father Duncan around 8:00 p.m. when he usually returned form his radio service. She was surprised to see a large crowd had gathered in his small house. The small living room had been converted to a makeshift meeting place. About 50 people were seated on the carpet, crowding the room. She noticed that there were quite a few Indians among the crowd. Part of the Indian community in Southern California, she thought.

At one end of the room, on a small platform, Father Duncan sat cross-legged in the traditional Indian style.

Around him were three Indian women dressed in saris. One, dressed in a simple white sari, was particularly pretty and striking. One of the women had a harmonium in front of her, the other two had what appeared to be a book of verses in front of them. The smell of Indian incense filled the room. When the crowd saw Kate entering, an excited murmur broke out. Father Duncan looked up, saw Kate, and motioned her to sit down. The crowd had parted to make way for Kate. Kate sat down and Father Duncan cleared his throat. The crowd fell silent.

"I welcome you all and particularly President Upshaw," began Father Duncan, "to this evening's rendition of verses from the Bhagavad Gita, the Divine Song. The Gita was conceived by great Indian sages thousands of years ago. Its message is as relevant today as it was when it was first created, perhaps even more so. The great men who created it have distilled the very essence of life into these immortal verses for the benefit of ordinary human beings. These verses teach us how to lead our lives on earth ever conscious of the soul within, but not ignoring the duties imposed on the corporeal body. They teach us how to retain our repose amidst disasters, preserve our equanimity in the presence of chaos. In short, it gives us the perfect message for our present predicament," he paused. "The eighteen chapters of the Gita contain hundreds of beautiful verses, each a gem of incomparable value.

"The setting for the Gita is a battlefield in ancient India. An internecine war is about to begin between the Pandavas, the rightful heirs to the throne of their father, and the Kauravas, their first cousins, who have unfairly usurped the throne. The greatest of the Pandava warriors is Arjuna, who, before the battle begins asks Krishna, his charioteer, to take him once around the amassed army of the Kauravas so that he may see his cousins, uncles and friends, one last time before he slays them. Arjuna is unaware that Krishna, his charioteer, is the very incarnation of Lord Vishnu, the supreme God. When Krishna drives Arjuna into the middle of the battlefield, Arjuna becomes unnerved at the sight of his cousins, his childhood friends, and other relatives, assembled there to fight. He throws down his bow and arrow, turns to Krishna and tells him that he doesn't want to fight, he doesn't want the kingdom, he cannot kill his own near and dear. Krishna, to calm Arjuna's nerves and to shake him out of his stupor, recites the Gita to him.

"The story and the characters are symbolic, meant to convey deeper, abstract, principles in a form more accessible to common people. Here, Pandavas represent all that is good and virtuous in man, Kauravas represent the evil, dark side of man, and the battlefield is the human brain where there is a constant struggle between good and evil thoughts to gain control of the body.

"The central message of the Gita is Karma Yoga, which can be roughly translated to mean the practice of detached action. To act, as your duty demands, without fear or expectation of the results that may ensue. It teaches that all external action is for the body, the soul itself is unperturbed by the actions, it merely observes the action without partaking in it. I believe that the message of the Gita, coupled with an unshakable Christian faith in God, is what we need at this time of uncertainty and anxiety. I have sought solace in it on many an occasion and it has never failed me. I hope you too shall find it as spiritually nourishing, as I have. Our Indian friends here," he pointed to the three women around him, "will sing the beautiful verses and explain their meaning for us. Starting today, we will sing 10 verses every evening until, Lord willing, we finish on land or on sea" he concluded.

The two women began singing the beautiful Sanskrit verses to the accompaniment of the harmonium. Kate listened, enraptured. They would sing a verse and then explain its meaning. It went on for three hours. At the end of the session, Kate was tired and hungry, but felt a calmness within that she had not felt in a long time.

After the crowd dispersed, Kate and the pretty young woman in white were the only ones left with Father Duncan. Father Duncan introduced her to Kate as Nilima Ray. She was doing her doctorate in philosophy at UCLA. She had been attracted to Father Duncan's services on TV and radio and come to him to offer help. They had then discovered their mutual love of the Gita and a strong bond had emerged.

Kate had dinner with Father Duncan and Nilima. After dinner, Father Duncan ushered the two of them into his office.

"Kate, do you mind if Nilima stays?" Father Duncan asked. "If you'd rather she leave, please don't hesitate to tell us."

"Of course, she can stay," said Kate. There was no particular harm in Nilima knowing her dilemma. She told them about how the speed of the landmass had been falling steadily in the past few days and had now become dangerously low, to the point where it was uncertain if they would make it to the Indian shore.

"What do you think Father," she asked, when she had finished with her description, "should I go on TV and explain the situation to the people, or should I stay mum?"

"They have a right to know Kate," the Father said. "Moreover, I believe it is their will and faith that is guiding us. I am positive their faith will be even stronger after they hear your news. That can only be for the better."

Nilima agreed with Father Duncan. They decided that Kate would address the people at 8:00 p.m. the next evening, after Father Duncan had had a chance to stress the need for even stronger faith in the final hours of their travail.

And so, the next day, Father Duncan introduced the Gita into his morning service. To his usual message of hope and faith, and his customary quotes from the Bible, he added at the very end, "As we approach India, it behooves us to pay heed to the message of the Bhagavad Gita, the Divine Song, the epitome of Hindu religious thought and philosophy. The Gita teaches us Karma Yoga, or action without attachment. It simply means do your righteous duty but don't worry about its consequences. Translated into our present context, it means do what you can to help the President, but don't waste your time worrying about what will happen to you. That is beyond your control. The President tells me that we are still 150 miles away from India. The Lord is taking us there, surely, but slowly. He wants our souls to ripen during this rite of passage. Remember, do not let your faith swerve. It is our faith that propels this ship. We maybe just one mile away from India, but if you lose your faith that will be one mile too many. Action without attachment and Christian faith. That's what will see us through." He repeated the same message on the evening radio service as well.

Kate addressed the people at 8:00 p.m. as planned. By then their speed had further fallen to about one and a half miles per hour. They were still about 140 miles away. She made her announcement calmly and dispassionately and urged them to heed the words of Father Duncan. No theatrics. No rhetoric. Simple, plain words. They had the desired impact. The people rallied around Father Duncan more than ever before. People came by The Church of Good Hope to personally express their support to Father Duncan. Kate's office got innumerable calls from people expressing solidarity and pledging unswerving faith.

It took them 7 days to reach India. Their speed fell to 1 mile per hour and held steady for 6 days. On the seventh day their speed began to fall even as they sighted the Indian peninsula. Dr. Sanders was in continuous touch with NASA and the reports came streaming. 0.75 miles per hour, 0.6...,0.5....,0.4...The last aerial survey made two hours before contact showed faint signs of jet stream activity, but no molten rock flow. As planned, all people had been evacuated from the coastal areas. As they sat watching in basements and emergency shelters with bated breath, the lucky ones watching the gap narrow, live on CNN, the crescent shaped landmass stretching from Santa Barbara to San Diego glided gracefully into Kanyakumari, or Cape Comorin as the British had named it, embracing the sharp point with its soft arch. Barely an impact was felt.

CHAPTER 18

*K*anyakumari, which in Sanskrit means unmarried maiden, the tautology in the name laying emphasis on the legend surrounding it, is one of the most spectacular and holy places in Southern India. Legend has it that thousands of years ago, Goddess Parvati, wishing to marry Lord Shiva, the foremost of the Hindu gods, came down to earth from heaven to do *tapas*, or severe penance in the form of meditation, to please Shiva. She was born as Kumari, a princess in a small southern kingdom at the tip of the peninsula. When Kumari came of age, she performed *tapas* and Lord Shiva came down to earth to answer her prayers. He came dressed as an ordinary man to marry her. Kumari agreed believing her prayers had been answered, and the wedding date was fixed. When Shiva came to the bride's house on the eve of the marriage with a wedding party, laden with wedding gifts, Kumari changed her mind. Unsure that it really was Lord Shiva, she declined to marry him. Enraged by her lack of faith, Shiva threw down the gold jewels, rubies, diamonds and other precious gifts, and walked away never to return. Kumari realized too late what she had done. She remained a Kanya, the Sanskrit term for an unmarried woman, forever, thus giving the place its name.

To this day, a temple dedicated to Goddess Parvati stands at land's edge, commemorating the legend. Its location at the point where the Arabian Sea, the Bay of Bengal and the Indian Ocean meet, is considered sacred by Hindus. It is also a place of spectacular beauty and from here one can watch breathtaking sunrises to the east and sunsets to the west.

Ten miles into the ocean, directly facing the temple, is a massive rock known as Vivekananda Rock. The rock is named after Swami Vivekananda, one of the greatest of Hindu philosophers and spiritual leaders, who brought the spiritualism of India to America in the late nineteenth century. The fabled Swami used to meditate on this rock and ever since it came to be known as the Vivekananda Rock. By fortunate happenstance, The Nation of Good Hope had missed the famous rock by a very narrow margin. San Diego had come to rest a few hundred feet from the rock, as if in obeisance to the great sage.

Three days after The Nation of Good Hope had landed, Kate stood staring in fascination at the idol of Kanyakumari, made of shiny black stone, dressed in a silk sari and bedecked with ornaments, flowers and other traditional Indian offerings of worship. She had not ventured out for two days. Despite the unexpectedly soft landing, their fears had not subsided. President Walters had assured her that he would do whatever she wanted, to help her. Prime Minister Dalal had called to reiterate his cooperation and offered assistance, again. A team of specialists from the Science Council, who had been waiting in India in anticipation of their arrival, had flown in to check for remnants of any jet stream activity and for traces of molten rock flow. They had all been extremely relieved to hear that there was no trace of jet stream activity, either horizontal or vertical. There was no trace of molten rock flow either. The water temperature all round was the customary 75 degrees Fahrenheit. Everything was normal. Yet they had a strange sense of anxiety. Not a soul had ventured out the first day to explore their new neighborhood. A fear of the unfamiliar and the unknown had gripped them.

On the second day after the landing, Kate had gone to visit Father Duncan. There she had met Father Duncan and Nilima, who had described with excitement the experience they had in the new land earlier during the day.

"Kate," Father Duncan had said, "you must see for yourself the beauty of this place. It's like nothing I've ever seen or experienced. It has a certain stillness and charm I cannot describe. Even as your eyes feast on the beauty without, your soul stirs to the beauty within. You feel the presence of the infinite."

"And the sunset! It is fantastic!" Nilima had gushed. She had not seen Kanyakumari earlier, either. Persuaded by them, Kate had gingerly ventured into this exotic land the next day. She had gone alone, not wanting anyone else to share her anxieties. And she had felt the ineffable charm from the moment she set foot on the Kanyakumari beach.

There were many points at which The Nation of Good Hope had land contact with the Indian peninsula. At some points just a few feet of water separated the two landmasses. At others, miles of water separated them. The largest gap was to the south of San Diego which was some 20 miles from the Indian shore. Where Kate stood, The Nation of Good Hope had literally fused into the Indian landmass, so one could step across the golden California sand, walk across parts of the ripped up Pacific Ocean floor, and onto the tricolored beach in front of the temple. The beach in Kanyakumari was famous for its colors. Red sand from the Arabian Sea to the west, black sand from the Bay of Bengal to the east, and the usual brown sand from the Indian

Ocean in the middle. To this was now added the golden hue of the sands of Southern California. For the first time in aeons, Goddess Kanyakumari had her gaze into the infinite interrupted by a new stretch of land that had come sailing in supplication to her feet.

Had Kate known the legend of Kanyakumari, the irony in this encounter would not have escaped her. Here she was, a woman spurned by what she had thought was her true love, staring at the Goddess, who had mistakenly rejected her only love and had in vain waited for thousands of years for him to return. The goddess had failed to win her lover back, would Kate succeed in replacing hers? She had not had a chance so far, but one would soon present itself.

"Hello!" said a friendly voice startling Kate out of her reverie. She turned around to see a tall man dressed in short sleeves and trousers, the tail of his shirt sticking out, staring pleasantly at her. "Do you realize you've desecrated the holy place?" he asked, pointing to her shoes. There was no menace or anger in his voice, just an understated humor. He was smiling.

Kate looked at her feet and at once realized what he meant. She knew Indians always removed their footwear before entering their house. She had not been to an Indian temple before, but of course, they wouldn't wear shoes inside a temple. "Oh!" she said, feeling silly. "I am sorry, I didn't realize ....I didn't mean any offense."

"Don't worry," he said pointing to the idol, "she's stood there many, many, years. She's seen stranger and more offensive things. Surely she'll forgive your faux paux. Hey, that's a good one! Faux paux! How appropriate!" His smile had broken into a grin.

149

Kate took a few minutes to realize the man was relishing his unintended pun. She broke into a laugh. "Good one, indeed!" she said, walking toward the entrance, her hand outstretched. "I'm Janet. Janet Merlin." She had instinctively lied about her name. She didn't want him to know who she was.

"I'm Hari Sharma. Call me Hari. Nice to meet you, Janet. May I call you Janet?"

Kate nodded. The man had an easy going charm. She had not been able to see him very well because of the darkness inside. But now, standing close to him, she realized he was handsome in a boyish way. He was tall and fair for an Indian. The wheatish smooth skin of his face shone, reflecting the radiance of youth and good health. The fresh shaven shade of blackish blue contrasted nicely with the rest of his face.

"You must be one of our new neighbors from Southern California," Hari said.

Kate nodded. He must be pretty well educated and well informed to know about Southern California, she thought. She couldn't resist asking, "How did you know?"

"That you are from Southern California? I read the papers you know. Biggest news in years. Besides, I lived there myself, for a few years."

This really fascinated Kate. She had floated close to 20000 miles, for more than six months, to run aground on a strange and foreign land, and the first person she runs into is from Southern California!

"What!" she exclaimed, "you must tell me about it."

"Oh, nothing much to talk about really. I'll tell you soon. But first, tell me, are you done admiring the goddess? Do you know her story? That's a lot more interesting than mine."

Kate nodded and then shook her head to indicate that she was done looking at the idol and no, she hadn't heard the story of the goddess. "I'd love to hear about it," she said. She found herself wanting to talk more to the pleasant young man.

Hari had been drinking Kate in. Kate, dressed in a pink spring dress and a straw hat to shield herself from the sun, looked fresh, charming and elegant.

"Sure. Let's step out and find a shady rock to sit on and I'll tell you."

They walked out onto the sunny beach. Hari took her to a small flat rock at the foot of a much larger one.

"This used to be my favorite place," he said, sitting on the small rock and resting his back against the large one. He motioned for Kate to sit next to him. "Used to be able to sit here and stare into the infinite beyond, where the waters blend into the sky. Perfect place for watching sunsets and sunrises, too. Did you know about the sunsets and sunrises in this place?"

Kate shook her head. "I heard about the sunsets, what about the sunrises?"

"Very unique. The only place of its kind I've heard of. This piece of land is at the very tip of the Indian peninsula, where the eastern shore meets the western shore. In the morning, you see the sun rise from the Bay of Bengal in the east. In the evening, you see it set into the Arabian Sea in the west. Absolutely fantastic. I've seen it for thirty-three years and it still takes my breath away, every time I see it."

So that's how old he was, Kate thought. Somehow, that little tidbit seemed more important than the sunrise or the sunset.

"I'm off on a tangent. You wanted to hear about the story of Kanyakumari," he said.

"The who?" asked Kate, not recognizing the name.

"Kanyakumari. The Goddess in the temple. Name means unmarried maiden. Typical Sanskrit tautological emphasis, you know."

Kate didn't, but nodded anyway. He proceeded to describe the story. He was a wonderful storyteller and described the story with animated gesticulations and variations of intonation, adding details of ancient Indian life so Kate's foreign senses could better imagine the setting for the story. Kate could practically see the young Kanyakumari in her mind's eye. She listened, completely engrossed.

After Hari was done, Kate sat silently looking into the sand, tracing patterns with her fingers. The story had made a tremendous impact on her. She was, of course, reminded of Peter and how he had walked away from her. She was taken aback by the eerie coincidence of listening to a story about sundered hearts from a handsome young man in an exotic land far removed from her familiar environs. How complete the coincidence would be if it turned out that he himself had suffered a similar romantic mishap as well, she was thinking to herself.

"Now tell me about you. What are you doing here?" she asked, more to take her mind away from what it had been preoccupied with.

"You are in a mood to chat, aren't you? Must have been boring and lonely, being out at sea for six months. But I thought you had 12 million people for company. Though, I imagine, it must have been tense and scary all the time."

Kate hadn't realized she was being inquisitive. But He was right. She hadn't felt relaxed, or discussed anything personal, with anyone for a long time. There had been no time. They had been obsessed with a single thought. Survival. This was the first time in months that she was chatting casually. After she had become the president, even her friends had maintained an awkward distance. The easy, familiar relationships had vanished. Even this man wouldn't be talking to her this way, if he knew who she was.

"I am sorry," she said, "didn't mean to probe. Just curious. You are the first Indian I've met in India, so I got carried away with my curiosity. And you are right, there was no time for shooting the breeze while we were at sea. It was awfully scary."

"No. No. Not at all," Hari said in a rush, "perfectly all right. I was just teasing. Not much to my story. I was born here. Grew up around here. Went to Madras to study engineering. Like most yong Indians with ambition, I too went to the U.S. for higher studies. Got my Ph.D. from M.I.T. Went to work with Pacific Aerospace in Southern California. Worked on advanced guided missiles. Left in 92 after the Desert Storm, when I saw first hand on TV what I was working to achieve. I've been here since. Catching up on Indian philosophy and literature. Saved enough from my sojourn in Southern California, so I don't have to work if I don't want to. Didn't imagine that Southern California would come right to my doorstep looking for me, though."

"Ph.D. from M.I.T.! Returns home after being disillusioned with defense systems! And you say there isn't much to your story. God! You Indians are understated."

"Generalizing from a sample of one. Isn't that dangerous? Anyway, now tell me about you."

"Me? Not as impressive as yours. Simple, Southern California girl. Grew up in an average middle-class family. All too typical American story. Abandoned by drunkard father. Scholarships and part time work paid my way through college. Graduated as an architect. Had a great job until this thing happened." She had left out the part about Peter, quite consciously. Maybe Hari had left out the bit about his romantic interlude too. Why should she confide in him?

It was 5:30 p.m. and she got up to go.

"It'll be sunset in about thirty minutes. It'll be a shame if you miss it. Wait a little longer and you won't regret it," Hari said.

Kate was starving. She hadn't had lunch. "I've got to go, I am famished," she said.

"Let's walk over to my house and I'll fix you something," Hari offered.

Kate hesitated. She had heard about the eating hazards in India. Hari sensed her hesitation.

"Don't worry, I know what you are thinking. I'll give you coffee and biscuits. That's pretty safe. Also, since you are going to be here for a while, I'll tell you something else. Indians are generally very clean and hygienic in their own homes. Outside, in the restaurants, it's another story."

"I'm sorry, I didn't mean it that way," Kate said, her face flushed.

"Quite all right. You must be careful what you eat. Stick to cooked food and you will be OK," Hari said.

They walked over to Hari's house. It was a sparsely furnished neat little cottage, just a few hundred feet from the temple. There were books everywhere. Books on literature, philosophy and religion, both western and Indian. All the famous western authors she had heard of were represented. There were many Indian ones she didn't recognize. She noticed several books in two unfamiliar languages.

"What books are those?" she asked.

"Classical Tamil and Sanskrit literature," he said, without elaborating.

It was clear he was very well read. Kate was impressed. After they had coffee and biscuits, they returned to the rock. The sun was lingering in the horizon, all red and aglow, ready to set. It was lovely.

"It used to be a lot better before," he said, "pointing to the buildings on the side of The Nation of Good Hope.

"I am sorry we spoilt it for you, but no one gave us a choice," Kate said.

They sat silently looking at the sun disappear into the water. It was suddenly dark.

"Twilight doesn't exist here," Hari explained, "it's light one minute and dark the next. Makes for a simple life. It's the twilight zone that complicates things." He was silent for a minute and then he continued, "What is going to happen next? What are you guys going to do?"

"We are not sure," Kate said, "most of us feel the last six months have changed our life fundamentally. We don't think we'd fit in if we went back to the United States. You've heard about what happened on The Nation of Good Hope, I'm sure."

"I have, and I was impressed beyond belief. What you guys pulled off was nothing short of incredible. Kate Upshaw and Father Duncan, they must be pretty amazing characters. I'd love to meet them. If only some such miracle could be worked here," he said with a sigh.

Kate was thrilled to hear his admiration for her. "I'm sure you can come over and meet them," she said and then she remembered the military guards that General Paterson had placed all around the border, and she said, "perhaps not right now, but soon enough, after things settle down a bit. What did you mean about a miracle being needed in India?"

"Oh, that's a long story. The shape this country's in, it's awful. It's a great country. Great heritage, cultural and spiritual. Talented people. Plenty of natural resources. Look at the condition we are in. First the British, and now our politicians. They are bleeding the country dry. The people have no chance to grow. If I start on this now, you'll end up seeing the sunrise too, I better stop. Tell you more later.

You better get going before it gets too dark. Will you be back tomorrow?"

"I don't know. I would like to. I'll try. I had a wonderful time. It was really nice meeting you. If not tomorrow, I'll drop by in the next couple of days. Bye."

Hari walked with Kate to the border and stood watching as she disappeared into the darkness. Kate had stirred him up quite a bit. The emotional tranquillity he had achieved with considerable effort had been disturbed again.

CHAPTER 19

Kate was very busy the next morning. She and her cabinet had a thousand things to worry about. Their problems now were entirely different. Their immediate danger had passed, but they couldn't relax. Their land was fundamentally unstable. There was no telling what could happen when. The ground could cave in any time anywhere. The experts from the Science Council were unsure if the landmass would ever stabilize geologically. Extensive studies of the submerged land off Los Angeles had shown that the breakaway landmass had crust varying in thickness from several thousand feet to tens of miles. The Science Council team could only guess as to why they had not seen any building collapses or felt any significant shock when The Nation of Good Hope had sailed into Kanyakumari. It was possible that the ocean floor off the Kanyakumari coast had the exact same gradient, only in the opposite direction, as that of the crust under the Nation of Good Hope, so that it fit perfectly like a wedge into its precut slot. That would be incredibly fantastic. The mathematical probability of that was infinitesimally small. Zero for all practical purposes.

Father Duncan would have offered a much simpler explanation. The Lord had intended it. This explanation would have been good enough for practically everybody on The Nation of Good Hope. They had simply been through too much to care for any other rational explanation. Faith alone had sustained them and the same faith that God had brought them to safety would have been good enough for them. But

Kate and her cabinet, while they shared the faith, could not assume everything was fine. They had a greater responsibility. They had to be absolutely sure. They didn't know if there still was a large amount of gas trapped underneath the surface. They didn't know if it was safe to drill a hole to test. Kate was getting tired of the unknowns. In the meantime, a lot of things they had pushed aside as not being important when they were in grave danger were now becoming important. Schools had remained closed for six months now. How much longer should they continue to be closed? When would it be safe for children to return? Unknowns again. Until the stability of the landmass could be determined, they could not take chances. President Walters had promised to send over a team of international experts to help them assess the situation. Until then they just had to wait.

And then there was also the issue of giving people the choice of staying or returning to America. Kate had discussed this with President Walters and, acting on his advice, had begun negotiations with Prime Minister Dalal for permission to build two runways large enough for jet planes to land, in Kanyakumari. President Walters had promised to send military transport planes to carry those who wanted to return to America. They had no idea how many people would choose to return. Even if only half chose to go back that would mean 6 million men, women and children and their pets. They could also begin evacuation by sea. Since they were unsure of the stability of the landmass, they could not afford to risk mass movement of people. They would have to designate hundreds of well separated evacuation points for evacuation by sea, and then transport people in carefully coordinated trips to the evacuation points.

General Paterson did some rough math. If they had two runways built in Kanyakumari, then assuming each runway could handle 24 flights a day, that would be 48 flights per day. If each plane carried 400 people, that was about 20000 people. If they had a 100 docking stations, and a 100 ships could simultaneously be loaded with people, then assuming each ship could carry an average of 1000 people, that would be 100000 people at a time. If they could load three ships per docking station per day, that would mean 300000 people could be evacuated by sea everyday. This gave a total of 320000 people evacuated by air and sea everyday. It would take 19 days to evacuate 6 million people, if everything went without a hitch. But General Paterson knew this simple minded math ignored an obvious hitch. This assumed they would have 300 ships each capable of carrying a thousand people, available every day for 19 days. That was a total of 5700 large ships. There probably weren't that many ships that size in the whole world. And there were other logistical issues like fuel for the ships, and so on. It was simply a nightmare. If 6 million people chose to return, in all probability it would take them something like six months. There was also the issue of the stability of the landmass. If it turned out to be unstable and uninhabitable, then most of the 12 million would return, barring the few who would opt to remain in India, assuming India would allow them to. In the worst case, to evacuate 12 million people, they would take up to a year. It was mind boggling.

As a first step, they decided that General Paterson would organize another door-to-door poll by the military to determine how many people wanted to return. They would then figure out the logistical details of evacuation. Before the poll, Kate would address the people to offer public thanks to God on their behalf and to explain their options.

Poor Hari had waited all day on his favorite rock for Kate. He had come prepared with a picnic basket containing biscuits, Indian snacks he had made himself, a thermos full of coffee and two napkins neatly folded. He had also brought along with him a carefully selected set of books, on philosophy, religion and literature, with which to impress Kate. All day long, the books had been spread around him nonchalantly. He had not read a single page. Neither had he opened the picnic basket. Finally, at 7:00 p.m., when it was too dark for Kate to come, he had given up hope and gone back to his cottage, hurt and disappointed. Kate, at that time, was addressing her people.

CHAPTER 20

*K*ate could not get away for another two days. Hari had been constantly on her mind. She felt a strong desire to see him. But there simply had been too much work. She was buried in meetings from early morning to late night, barely finding time to eat.

On the third day, as soon she got a chance, she slipped out to see Hari. She crossed over to the Kanyakumari beach and went straight to Hari's rock. He wasn't there. She went to the temple, carefully removed her shoes, and went in to search. He wasn't there either. She walked up and down the beach. Not a sign of another human being. She decided to check his house. She walked over to the cottage and knocked. There was no answer. She knocked again. Again, no answer. She waited a while and knocked for the third time. No answer. She turned around and headed back in disappointment. She had barely taken three steps when she heard a hoarse cry, "Kate!" She looked back, Hari was at the door of his cottage dressed in crumpled white pajamas and a white kurta.

She was shocked at his appearance. She could barely recognize him. He was unshaven, his eyes red and swollen. He looked sick. She ran to him shouting, "Hari! What's the matter?" Suddenly, she stopped short. *He had called her Kate. He knew*. She walked over to him slowly.

"Kate, you are here! I didn't think you would come," Hari's voice was weak.

She walked up to him and touched his forehead. It was warm. "How did you find out?" she asked.

Hari pointed to a newspaper clipping lying on the floor. It showed a large picture of Kate, smiling and waving.

After Hari had returned home disappointed that Kate hadn't come, he had leafed through his old newspapers looking for some information on Janet Merlin. He had vaguely remembered seeing her face. What he had found instead was Kate. He had then felt terribly let down, first because Kate had lied to him about her identity, and second, because she was Kate. Kate Upshaw, the President. The most famous woman in the world. He had given up hope of ever meeting her again. He hadn't slept all night and the next morning when he woke up he had felt feverish. The fever had continued for the next two days. Of course, he didn't tell Kate the whole story, just the bare outline. However, Kate had no trouble filling in the blanks. She had correctly guessed what had happened.

In the meantime, his insouciance had returned and he was trying to make light of the whole thing. "Just a mild fever. Will be gone by the end of the day. Happens all the time in these parts. It is the cool wind that blows sometimes at night. If you are sleeping without your shirt and it catches you in the chest, you are sure to come down," he said.

He made Kate sit down, apologizing profusely for the mess. When he came back twenty minutes later, he looked his former self. His clean shaven face looked almost healthy, except for the redness in his eyes. He was dressed in shirt and trousers.

"Should I call you Ms. President?" he asked, only half jokingly.

Kate looked at him, frowning. "Hari," she said,"I'll tell you why I lied to you and then we'll be even. I thought if I told you who I am, that would put you off. I didn't want that. So call me Kate, unless you lied to me too and you are really Prime Minister Dalal and not Hari. In that case, I am Madam President to you."

They both laughed heartily. The awkwardness was gone, its place taken by an undefined warmth.

They talked the whole day sitting on the rock. And the next. And the next... It became a secret routine of Kate's to slip out whenever she could. She would always find Hari waiting for her on his rock. On their rock. They had spent so much time together on it that it had now become their rock. There was not a subject on earth they didn't talk about. World affairs, life in America, life in India, religion, philosophy, about Kate, about Hari, about The Nation of Good Hope, everything. Kate had been quite impressed by his depth and breadth, his keen intellect and sharp, sometimes mordant, sense of humor, and above all by his deep affection and caring for her. He had been attracted to her freshness, youthful vivacity, the can-do attitude, charm, and honesty. They had fallen deeply in love. Over a period of three weeks or so, Kate had discovered Hari's multifaceted personality.

Once, talking about her experience while at sea, Kate had told Hari, "It was simple faith that got us through Hari. The Science Council, with the best scientific minds in America, could not help us. But Father Duncan with his simple message of faith and hope gave us the strength to get through."

To which Hari had replied, "Kate, it is a popular myth that science has answers to everything. The fact is that science has answers to nothing. Some branches of science have approximate answers to approximate questions, while others have exact answers to approximate questions. There is no branch of science that has exact answers to exact questions."

Kate had not followed. "What do you mean Hari? Are you saying two plus two equals four is not an exact answer?" she had asked, puzzled.

"It is an exact answer, Kate. But what is the question? You know what Einstein said about Mathematics? He said, 'Mathematics is exact, but has no content'. So much for the queen of sciences. Physics, on the other hand, has a lot of content, but how exact is it? Utterly and completely approximate. The more you know about Physics, the less you understand. I was perfectly happy in high school to understand the world through Newton's Laws. Then in college they told us Newton's Laws were approximate, but Einstein's theories were exact. Later, I learned that Einstein's theories are approximate too. Now I believe that all science is empirical. Some theorists turn their noses up at experimentalists. But what about them? What are their theories explaining? Just their assumptions. And Godel showed us that there can never be a completely consistent set of assumptions; there will always be exceptions. Only faith in God can give you the experience of exactness. Absolute exactness, absolute truth, God, they are all the same."

"You do believe in God, then?" Kate had asked.

"You really have no choice, Kate. Whether you call it God or not, what science cannot explain but the human mind can experience, I call God. Someone else may have a simpler definition. To him God may just be Shiva, or that

165

idol," he had pointed to the temple, "or Christ. But the concept is the same."

"So are you defining God as the absence of something?" Kate had persisted.

"At this level of abstraction, the absence of something is the same as the presence of something else. The absence of a scientific explanation of things observed in nature leads to a belief, or faith, which is God. Maybe this example will make it clearer. You know the transcendental number pi, it is the ratio of the circumference of a circle to its diameter. Any high school kid knows this. Now, suppose you didn't know what pi was. You had just heard about it and you are trying to figure out what it is. Someone throws one of those infinite series expansions of pi at you and says "There! that's pi." Each time you find a new term of the infinite series, you exclaim 'Aha! now I know what pi is!' until you find the next term, and the next term, and so on. To ancient Greeks and Indians, pi was twenty-two divided by seven. Later, the Chinese thought it was 3.14. Someone else found it was 3.14159. Now, modern computers can calculate pi to millions of decimal places. Some kid in Japan has memorized pi to the thousandth decimal place, or some such thing. Now, if they didn't relate pi to a circle, would knowing pi to a million places help them understand pi any better? I don't think so. God is like pi, and science is like an infinite series expansion of pi. It keeps finding new terms, but will never understand pi. You've got to have faith in the circle of life to understand the pi of God."

"We know a circle exists. Every circle has a circumference and a diameter. So we can define pi. If somebody wants proof, I will draw a circle, draw a diameter, ask him to divide the circumference by the diameter, and there you have the proof that pi exists. How will you prove that God exists?" Kate had challenged.

"A very good question, Kate. One that had puzzled me for a very long time. I will give you the answer a Swamiji once gave me. Let us say the defining characteristic of God is omnipresence. God is present in everything and everything is present in God. All major religions, Hinduism, Christianity, they all say this, right? OK now, let me give an example of something that has these properties. Space. The whole universe is in space, and space is in everything. Until someone finds the smallest possible subatomic particle, this must be true. If somebody proves to me that they found the smallest subatomic particle possible, then I'll accept there is no God. Until then the argument that space exists, so God must exist, is good enough for me. Admittedly the space analogy applies to just one facet of God, but isn't it amazing that we can have some intuitive understanding of even one facet? Who knows, with the right level of enlightenment one maybe able to appreciate the other aspects of God as well. At least I can now imagine what great souls like Christ and Buddha probably experienced."

This rationale that God must exist had been an eye-opener to Kate, had somehow appealed to her precise, engineering mind and had enhanced the intuitive faith that was inherent in her and had been nurtured by Father Duncan.

Hari's was a complex personality. He could be earnestly arguing about something dead serious one minute, and be riproaringly funny, the next. Once Kate had asked him for his views on arranged marriage, something that she had found fascinating about India even while she was in America.

"Let me give you a man's perspective," Hari had said, "don't get me wrong, I'm not sexist. But I can best explain it from a man's perspective. In an arranged marriage, a new wife is like a new pair of jeans. In the beginning you are quite uncomfortable and there is a lot of getting used to. Gradually it begins to fit better and then it sticks close to you, and the more it fades, the better it fits. A new wife in a love marriage is like a new, red, sports car. In the beginning it is all slick and shiny and you love the performance. You dote on the car. Pretty soon you start noticing nicks here and scratches there, the body isn't great any more. A couple of years later you realize the performance is not so hot either, other cars are passing you on the road. That's when you start thinking of a newer, redder and sportier car. This is, of course, an oversimplification. Sure, you can be stuck with jeans that are not the right size for you, or not properly tailored, and, sure, you'll see a man with the same red, sports car all his life because he loves that car and doesn't want another fancier one. But you get the picture."

Kate had laughed till her sides ached. That was the most accurate, if exaggerated, and hilarious summary she had ever heard on that subject. And she related to the description on a personal level too. She had been a red sports car herself and was now more inclined towards being a new pair of jeans.

Kate had learned that Hari entertained traditional Indian views on sex and marriage. He believed that premarital sex is fundamentally wrong because it was irresponsible. What would happen to the baby, should the woman conceive and the couple decided not to get married? Maybe they had a right to indulge themselves sexually, but what right did they have to mess up the kid's life? None. So the logical inference, then, was that until you are prepared to commit to each other permanently, a couple had no right to have sex.

Kate had learned of his views the hard way. Once, coming to see him in the evening, she had found him alone, sitting on the beach, leaning back on his arms, feet stretched out, his hair dancing in the cool breeze. She had found him irresistibly handsome and had felt the urge to hold him tightly. She had sneaked silently from behind, put her arms around him, and hugged him. Hari had involuntarily recoiled from her, pushing her away. Somewhat hurt, but more puzzled, she had walked away in a huff. Hari had come running to her singing an improvised love limerick, borrowing from Kipling's famous poem, "For east is east and west is west, And never the twain shall meet."

By then he had caught up with her, turned her around, kissed her on the mouth and continued, "But if they do, oh! what a treat, The joy of it, just can't be beat."

After that, there was no way Kate could continue to feel angry. She had, in fact, been aroused and returned his kiss passionately. Hari had, after a while, gently pushed her away saying, "No Kate, not now. Let's wait. I prefer the Indian way," and then he had launched into a lengthy discourse on his views on premarital sex. As usual, Kate had come away, agreeing with him.

After three weeks of intense courting, they were madly in love with each other. Neither had ever felt happier.

CHAPTER 21

*E*ver since the Military Police sergeant had brought him word about Kate's clandestine meetings with Hari, General Patterson had been agitated. He didn't quite know how to react. He really was in two minds. His first reaction was one of shock, even horror. That a head of state could carry on a covert affair at a time of great uncertainty was indeed upsetting to his military mind. However, he had by now come to know Kate intimately. He knew her family story, how her father had dumped them all when Kate was still very small, and how, later, Peter had left her without warning. He really admired Kate for the courage she had shown and the leadership she had provided throughout the yearlong crisis they had endured. He could understand how terribly lonely her private life must have been under these circumstances. It was natural that she desired a man's company. But still, how could he accept that she was sneaking off every day spending so much time with a common Indian. If unchecked, where would that lead? Would it be a threat to the security of The Nation of Good Hope? The answer was not clear. He needed to talk this over with other senior people. He didn't feel comfortable talking to the Cabinet members. The matter was too sensitive. Kate was immensely popular and he didn't want to discuss a delicate subject, one on which he was not even sure where he stood, with Kate's Cabinet. He just didn't know them well enough. He decided his best option was to call a meeting with General Garland and

Admiral Tyson. He could trust them. They could have an open discussion, view the matter objectively, and come to the right conclusion. Once they formed a consensus view, they could share it with the Cabinet. He asked his aide to set up a private meeting at 2:00 p.m. that same afternoon with General Garland and admiral Tyson.

General Garland and Admiral Tyson both arrived at 2:00 p.m. sharp. General Patterson greeted them warmly. Once they had settled in comfortably, each with his favorite whiskey and soda, General Patterson began, "Gentlemen," he said, "what I am about to tell you should be considered classified information of the highest order," he saw the surprised looks on their faces, they had not expected anything remotely like this, but he continued without stopping, "some information has been brought to my attention that concerns me greatly. I am not quite sure what to make of it. I need your help," he paused. They looked at him quizzically. "You may have noticed," he continued, "that the President has been missing for long periods, several hours at a time, in the last few weeks." They nodded. They had noticed, as had every member of the Cabinet and Kate's personal staff.

"You may recall the time when the President's personal assistant made frantic calls to each of us because President Walters was on the line." They nodded again. "And what did President Upshaw tell us? That she had gone on a long walk to clear her head. Well, she was not lying. Not entirely. Turns out, she did go on a walk, but not to clear her head. She has been visiting this Indian guy across the border. And from the looks of it, it is more than a casual meeting. Much more." He could see the shocked expressions on their faces.

171

"Who is this guy? How did she run into him?" Admiral Tyson asked.

"I don't think she knew him from before. I think it is a chance encounter. His name is Hari. And here's the surprising bit. He used to live in Southern California. He used to work for Pacific Aerospace," he paused. The Military Police had done their homework and dug into Hari's background. "This is the part that worries me, he quit Pacific Aerospace and came back to India after the Gulf War in 92. Apparently he didn't like what we did there. Who knows what classified information he had access to, and what he has been up to in India since his return? Could it be just a coincidence that he ran into President Upshaw, or is it part of a carefully thought out plan? I am not sure. It worries the hell out of me. We've hardly been here three weeks. Our future is not at all certain. We don't know how our relationship with India will shape up. Both President Walters and Prime Minister Dalal have given us their assurance and extended full support. The Prime Minister has gone above and beyond what we could have expected. He has deployed the Indian military all along our border with India to ensure that there are no incursions. All that is well and good, but the fact remains that things are far from settled. The next few months are vital in terms of determining our future. At a time like this to have President Upshaw distracted and unfocused is disturbing to say the least. What do we do about her Indian boyfriend? How do we deal with this thorny issue?"

"This is a tricky issue," Admiral Tyson said, "we can't barge into President Upshaw's private life. On the other hand, we cannot ignore any potential threats to national security. Can we get more information on this guy, Hari? Find out more about his background. What he's been up to in India since he came back. That'll tell us whether we should be worried about this, or leave the President alone to deal with her personal business."

"That's a good idea. May be we can contact someone in America. But we have to be careful. We all know how President Walters feels about our President. She's like a daughter to him. If he finds out we're probing around, he will be really upset at us," General Patterson said. He too liked Kate as a person and a friend. It bothered him that he had to go behind her back, but what choice did he have? The stakes were just too high.

"I know just the right person for you. Jack Kent. He is the CIA Director. I hear he hasn't been very happy about how things have turned out for us. He was rather hoping that we'd all end up at the bottom of the Pacific along with all the advanced defense equipment and classified information. This has been a sore disappointment to him, so if there is any dirt he can unearth on any one here, he'll only be too happy to share it," General Garland said.

"That's a great idea," General Patterson said, "I too have heard about the plans he had in mind for us. Like getting rid of our military equipment even if it meant risking volcanic explosions when we were drifting along on the Pacific not knowing how long we would keep floating or when we would sink. He is one self-serving bastard. Doesn't give a shit what others think or need. He's just the man for us to dig up some info on this guy, Hari. Let me see what I can get from him and then let's get back and discuss. Until then this is all hush-hush. Keep it under wraps. No one else should hear a word about it." The meeting wound up. They all shook hands and Admiral Tyson and General Garland left.

General Patterson didn't waste any time. It was the middle of the night in Washington D.C., but he didn't care. He asked his aide to track down Jack Kent's private number and place a call. General Patterson had no idea, but he was playing right into Jack Kent's hands. Jack Kent had already been informed about Kate and Hari. His elaborate CIA network in India had found out about Kate's relationship with Hari and alerted him nearly two weeks ago. In the beginning, Jack Kent had been mildly amused. But as the frequency of Kate's meetings with Hari grew, he had had become increasingly concerned. This was getting too serious for his liking. And when he found out that Hari used to work for Pacific Aerospace and left America after the Gulf war unhappy and disgruntled, he nearly blew a lid. He asked his agent in Madras, in south India, to keep tabs on Kate and Hari and to alert him immediately if he noticed anything unusual.

In the months after President Walters had cleverly engineered the separation of The Nation of Good Hope, Jack Kent had learned the full story about how President Walters had been in on it from the beginning and had pulled the wool over their eyes. He had been enraged. His first instinct had been to leak it to the press. But a fine intuition for self preservation gained over years spent practicing the subtle art of subterfuge that he specialized in, had stopped him. President Walters' popularity was so high, and he had become such a towering world figure in the aftermath of the statesmanship he had displayed in protecting The nation of Good Hope, that no newspaper of repute would have touched the story. And even if they did, what was the use? The deed was done. The Nation of Good Hope was a new, free, country floating further and further away from mainland USA carrying with it its precious defense cargo and military secrets. That was a fait accompli and nothing could be done about it. He would wait for his opportunity, he had decided.

General Patterson's call was just the opportunity Jack Kent had been waiting for all these months. When he got the call, Jack Kent was wide awake, going over some intelligence dossiers. "Hello," he said, angry at being called that late in the night, "do you realize what time it is?"

"Sorry, sir. Really sorry to disturb you. This is General Patterson's aide. He wants to speak to you about something urgent." Kent's trained mind knew in a flash what the General's call was about. Feigning sleepiness, he yawned and said, "Quite alright. Put the General through." General Patterson came on the line. "Hello Mr. Kent, I apologize for disturbing you at this late hour, but I needed to talk to you on a matter of some urgency."

"No problem at all General," said Kent, yawning conspicuously, "I am used to these late night calls. Especially, given the situation you are in, I'd drop anything to take a call from you." Knowing Jack Kent's reputation fully well, General Patterson was still impressed.

"Thank you Mr. Kent. Really appreciate it. Can I discuss something with you off the record and in strict confidence?"

"Of course, General. You have my word."

"It's about President Upshaw."

"You can trust me completely General."

General Patterson described to Kent how Kate had been meeting the Indian, Hari, crossing the border and spending hours at a time with him. He explained how concerned he and the other military leaders were about this. Particularly given Hari's past history with Pacific Aerospace.

"We didn't know how to deal with this. We need to find out more about this guy, Hari. What he's been up to in India since he returned. Does he have any defense connections with India or other countries? What are his current feelings about America? We know he left America feeling bitter and disappointed with the Gulf war. Does it mean he is anti-American? If so, is all this a plot to con President Upshaw in order to gain access to the military equipment and the defense secrets? We need your help to figure all this out. I am sure you have an extensive network here. Can you help us?"

Jack Kent was thrilled. This was just what the doctor had ordered. "Absolutely, General. This is right up my alley. We have extensive presence in India. All the way up to the highest levels of government. Give me a day or two and I'll get back to you with everything we can find on Hari."

"Mr. Kent, we want this done without anyone else finding out anything about it. Including President Walters. Can you manage that?"

"Certainly, General. I perfectly understand your situation. I'll be very discreet."

"Thank you, Mr. Kent. Much depends on the information you come back with. This could be a sinister plot or a perfectly innocent affair between two young people. Good night, and again, sorry for disturbing you in the middle of your sleep."

"Not at all, General. Good night."

Jack Kent did absolutely nothing to follow up on General Patterson's request. He just sat tight for the next two days. He already knew everything there was to know about Hari, which was nothing. Absolutely nothing. Hari had left America to get away from defense related work. He had spent all his time on the Kanyakumari beach reading philosophy and literature and pondering about life and its meaning. Of course, Kent didn't know this, but he knew Hari had no connection to any defense related matter to do with India or any other country.

It is common knowledge that CIA has had an active presence on the Indian subcontinent from before the time India got its independence from the British. In its earlier incarnation, it had been known as the Office of Strategic Services. After India gained independence, CIA became quite active in India. India's first Prime Minister, Nehru, was firm about India being nonaligned and remaining neutral in the cold war between America and Russia. India had close military ties with Russia, but continued its close relationship with England, and to a lesser extent, other European countries. Its relationship with America had been somewhat strained, but not hostile. CIA had penetrated the Indian Government to the highest levels and, among other things, was fully informed of all the defense deals. In the eighties and nineties there had been several scandals involving defense deals with France, Sweden and other European countries implicating several high ranking Indian civil and military officers, including Cabinet level ministers. CIA was completely aware of all this. It had a fine tuned network that was quite well plugged into the Indian defense machinery. As a result, Jack Kent didn't even have to ask for any specific information to be sent to him. He already knew the salient facts and all the key players involved. Just to be sure, he directed the India cell

177

in the CIA headquarters to find out if Hari had links with the Indian Government or the Indian defense industry. The answer was an emphatic no.

Two days later Jack Kent called General Patterson. "I am afraid I have bad news for you General Patterson," he said, "it is just as you had feared. Hari is a disgruntled guy. He hates America. He thinks we are evil and we are out to destroy the world with our missiles and nuclear arms. He has connections high up in the Indian Government. We don't have all the details yet, but we think he is trying to gain access to President Upshaw hoping to acquire defense secrets. May be even steal some of the advanced military equipment."

"Oh my God!" General Patterson said, "this is terrible. It is much worse than we thought. We must warn President Upshaw. The poor woman, to be twice deceived by a man after being dumped by her own father. She will hate all men after this."

"I am sorry General, I know how you feel about President Upshaw. But it is pretty bad. We don't have a choice. You must confront her, explain how dire the situation is and ask her never to see that man again," Kent said. "And one more,thing. Please don't disclose to anyone outside of your military circle that I gave you this information. CIA already gets a bad rap, and if it becomes known that CIA is the source for this information, our work in the Indian subcontinent will become much harder."

"I understand, Mr. Kent. Admiral Tyson and General Garland are already aware that I am talking to you about this issue. I assure you that outside of them no one else will know that you gave me this information. And, by the same token, I want your assurance that this will remain strictly between you and me. No one else should hear about it."

Jack Kent gave his word and they hung up.

General Patterson was quite upset and genuinely concerned for Kate. This would be shattering for her. There was no way they could let her continue to meet Hari. They would have to put the breaks on that. He would have to discuss the details with General Garland and Admiral Tyson, but the course of action was pretty clear.

When the three military leaders met the next morning, they very quickly agreed that Kate had to break with Hari. They had to let her know right away. The security of The Nation of Good Hope was at stake. Its very existence may be threatened if they didn't implement proper safeguards. It was decided that General Patterson would have a private meeting with Kate, give her the information about Hari and convince her to stop seeing him. The thought never occurred to them that Kate may not believe their information, or even if she did believe, that she may refuse to break up with Hari. They had such implicit faith in her.

As soon as the other two left, General Patterson called Kate's office. It was a relatively quiet morning and he happened to catch Kate alone in her office without any meetings. Kate was both surprised and delighted to hear General Patterson's voice on the phone. It had been a couple of weeks since she had talked to him.

"Oh General! It is so nice to hear from you. It's been a while," she said.

"Yes, Kate, I know. Too long. How are you? I know you've been busy like hell with all the discussions with the Indian Government and President Walters and the White House staff. Figuring out all the details about how to transition to normalcy can't be easy."

"Yes, General. It is overwhelming. So many things to think of. The economy, water, gas, electricity, food, defense, foreign policy, security,.....sometimes it feels like life was easier when we were drifting aimlessly in the Pacific."

"Don't say that Kate. You know that's not true. Each minute of that ordeal was unbelievably tense. Yes, the details you have to deal with now are overwhelming. But you have the full support of President Walters. He has got Congress to approve virtually unlimited aid to take care of all our financial needs. And Prime Minister Dalal has been so cooperative. We are all here to help you." He got so caught up in the conversation he almost forgot the purpose of his call. He suddenly realized that he was veering off topic and he said, "Kate, are you free tonight? Can we meet at the Officers' Club for dinner? I have some things I want to talk to you in private. No one will bother us there, we can have dinner in my private dining room and talk freely."

"Sure General, but you sound anxious. I hope this is nothing affecting you personally."

"No, nothing like that. Just that so much has happened in the past three weeks and we've all been so busy. I want to catch up with you. Tell you what I've seen and heard and find out what your impressions are. That's all. I could easily have driven over to your office and met you for dinner there. But the chances of you being left alone to eat and chat in peace are pretty small. That's why I thought you coming over here would be better. No one will bother us here."

Kate realized immediately that it must be pretty important stuff he wanted to discuss since he was asking her to drive quite a long way to ensure an uninterrupted dinner meeting. They agreed to meet for dinner at 6:30 p.m. at the Officers' Club.

When Kate drove over to the Army Officers' Club in the evening she found General Patterson's aide waiting for her outside. As they walked through the entrance, they caused quite a stir among the Army officers they passed. Several of them came running to Kate, saluted and shook hands. Kate smiled at them warmly but walked on without lingering to talk.

The aide ushered Kate into General Patterson's dining room. The dining room was elegantly appointed. It had been designed to impress upon the guests the fact that their host was the highest ranking military officer in Southern California. It was unusually large for a dining room and was soundproofed. General Patterson had established a strict protocol, so no one entered the room unless summoned by a bell. And even then, they had to knock on the door before entering. General Patterson used this dining room for entertaining high ranking visitors and for particularly sensitive meetings over lunch or dinner, so the staff knew that every occasion there was special and treated it accordingly. They had never hosted the President before, so there was an extra buzz. All the staff had changed into freshly starched and ironed uniforms and they had attentive, eager, expectant, expressions on their faces. After welcoming Kate they discreetly withdrew. General Patterson saw Kate, got up, walked towards her and gave her a warm hug. He noticed a new glow on her face.

"I am glad you could come, Kate. So nice to see you," he said.

Kate returned his hug and said, "I am looking forward to the dinner General. I hear your chef is one of the best in Southern California.....well, I mean The Nation of Good Hope." They both laughed at her inadvertent slip.

"Yes, he was one of the best in Southern California and he is undoubtedly the best here," General Patterson said.

"I haven't talked to you in nearly two weeks. What have you been up to General? I know you were concerned about our border with India."

"We have taken good precautions. We have both the MPs and Border Security patrolling the border with India as well as the coastal area on the Indian Ocean side. So far so good. Luckily, Prime Minister Dalal has deployed the Indian military and sealed off access to us on the Indian side. He has given strict orders and they are enforcing it scrupulously. Only locals are being allowed into our immediate vicinity. There is a fifty mile zone of separation all around. No nonlocals are allowed to enter this zone. This has helped a great deal. The locals are mostly superstitious village folk. They have stayed away from the border, apparently it is bad luck to sight us. A stroke of good luck for us," he said, grinning. He was doing his best to look and act normal. He was doing a great job of concealing the anxiety he felt.

"That's great to hear. One less headache for us. Though, this state of affairs cannot continue for long. Once we figure out the exact nature of our situation, how we are going to interact with India, what we need from them, what will they expect from us, etc., we need to come up with a border policy. But we have time for all that, we can work out these details over time," Kate said.

The waiter brought them the menu. The chef had prepared a special treat. It was fusion food. A unique blend of Southern California herbs and vegetables and South Indian spices. They had vegetable fritters for appetizers and curried rice, lightly fried chicken, spicy goat meat and unleavened Indian bread, Chapati, for the main course. For dessert they had a traditional South Indian pudding called Payasam. The food was delicious. Kate ate heartily. She didn't notice that General Patterson wasn't enjoying the outstanding food with quite the same relish she was.

Right through dinner Kate had been doing most of the talking. There were a whole slew of issues confronting her and she was happy she had a chance to sound them out with the General. She talked about the economy, transitioning The Nation of Good Hope from what was essentially a very large commune to a modern industrial economy, was a thorny issue. They had to do it without disturbing the deep communal harmony and the closeness people had developed and come to cherish. They had to migrate what had become a good faith based barter economy to a monetary economy. They could never go back to the old purely capitalist economy, it would have to have a strong socialist element. Something along the lines of what the Scandinavian countries had. Except there's was not a homogeneous society, it was very mixed. The whites were in fact barely a majority. This would add further challenges. They would require the infusion of large amounts of cash. President Walters had gotten a generous aid package approved by Congress. They had to figure out the best monetary policy and the best way to use the American aid. Kate was happy to get General Patterson's thoughts on all these issues. They got so caught up in the discussions that General Patterson even forgot about Hari for the time being. The excellent Napa Valley wine no doubt played a part in quelling his anxiety. They were done with dinner and having coffee when General Patterson realized with a start that he needed to bring up the matter of Hari.

"It's a lot to worry about Kate. And it's quite exciting too. We have a totally fresh start to make. This is unprecedented in history. You have all the resources you need and the full freedom to spell out national policy on everything from the economy to defense to foreign policy, health, social services,... everything. You have an excellent Cabinet. And the people are solidly behind you. Take your time, don't rush into it. Get peoples' opinions through referendums, where needed. It is absolutely essential to keep them involved and to ensure they have a big stake in all the major decisions. Their faith and support got us this far. We still need the same fervor and commitment from them to give the right shape and structure to our country. I am sure you'll figure it out. I'll be right along side helping you with defense, military and border issues," General Patterson paused. He looked at Kate. She seemed happy and totally relaxed. "I have to do it now," he thought to himself, "it is getting late and she'll want to leave soon."

"Kate, there is something else I wanted to talk to you about. A private thing," he said.

"What is it General? I trust your family is fine," Kate said, expressing concern.

"My family is fine, Kate. Thanks for asking. I was one of the lucky few whose immediate family survived this disaster intact. I have plenty of people in mainland USA, of course, but my wife and kids are right here with me. Actually, it's about you."

"Me?" Kate was visibly surprised.

"Yes, I don't quite know how to bring it up. It is embarrassing for me, I am not used to these situations."

"What situations, General? We've been through so much together. You can tell me anything. In this room I am not President Upshaw, I am Kate."

"Thank you, Kate. The trust you place in me both makes my job easier and harder at the same time. It has to do with Hari."

"What! What about Hari? How do you even know about him?"

"I was alerted by the MP, Kate. They told me you've been meeting him practically every day for the last three weeks. And there were occasions when you were urgently needed and nobody could find you."

Kate blushed in embarrassment. She, of course, remembered the call from President Walters that she had missed.

"I know this is your private business, Kate. And I respect it. But you are our President and it is our duty to protect you. The news about Hari is not good, Kate."

Kate was shocked. "What do you mean, General, what do you mean not good? What have you heard that's negative?" Her face had turned an angry red and her voice had grown louder.

"What I am going to tell you now is very reliable information, Kate. Hari is part of an elaborate plan to infiltrate The Nation of Good Hope and acquire our defense information. Possibly even steal our military equipment. Hari is a spy. He either works for the Indian Government or for one of the defense contractors, we are not yet sure. But you do know that Hari is from Southern California and he used to work for Pacific Aerospace?" He looked at Kate.

Kate's cool, calm, composure had abandoned her. The color had drained from her face. Suddenly, the youthful freshness was gone, replaced by a confused, scared and angry look. "Hari made no secret of it General, that's the first thing he told me," she said.

"That's often how it happens, Kate. They tell you something important to earn your trust. But it is not the full story. You know he left the U.S. after the Desert storm? He….," Kate didn't let him finish.

"Yes, he told me that too. He was disappointed and disillusioned. Didn't want his intellectual efforts going into killing innocent people. What's wrong with that, General? Remember the Iraqi soldiers who were strafed on the highway returning from Kuwait to Baghdad? They were sitting ducks, General," Kate was angry.

"I know Kate. I am not proud of that. I am not defending that action. My point was not that we were right. It is simply that it turned Hari against America. He is convinced we are evil. Out to destroy the world with our missiles and nuclear arms. He has completely forgotten about everything America did after the fall of Saddam Hussein. We spent hundreds of billions of dollars and lost thousands of soldiers. We still haven't succeeded in establishing a stable Iraqi government. But it is not for lack of trying. He's forgotten all that, or he has chosen to ignore it. He is so embittered, he can only think in one direction. American military capability is harmful and must be stopped. Trust me, I have this information from highly reliable sources. He has worked very hard to get close to you Kate."

All this was too much for Kate. She felt a dizzy sensation. Her mind had wandered off to her first meeting with Hari. Had he followed her to the temple of Kanyakumari? And that charming story he had told her about the legend of Kanyakumari, had he planned it all knowing her break-up with Peter? Had he simply gone along with her when she had introduced herself as Janet Merlin? The next time she went to see him he had told her he had discovered she was Kate, and he was so upset at her. Was that all an elaborate set up? What about all the discussions on religion, philosophy, sex – even refusing sex? The many intimate moments they had spent together. Had it all meant nothing? She didn't want to believe it. She didn't know what to do. Tears started streaming down her face. General Patterson got up and walked over to her side, bent down, put his arms around her and said, "I am so sorry Kate. I hate myself for doing this to you. Especially after everything you've been through. But I had no choice."

Kate said nothing. She was sobbing now, resting her head on General Patterson's shoulders. General Patterson stroked her back gently. After a while Kate recovered partially, lifted her head up, looked at General Patterson and asked, "What should I do General?"

"Make a clean break and put an end to it, Kate. Stop seeing him. He'll get the message. The good thing is we nipped it in the bud, no harm done."

"It is easy for a man who has the comfort of his family around him to say that General. No harm done! Do you have any idea how it feels to go back to my lonely little house every night?" she lashed out.

"Kate, I am sorry. I didn't mean it that way. What I meant was that the nation's security has not been compromised. What's happened with you at a personal level is terrible. But we have no choice, you cannot let it continue."

"You are sure about this information General? Where did you get it from? How do you know there is no conspiracy there?"

"As sure as I can possibly be, Kate. It comes from an impeccable source. I can't tell you who it is because I have given by commitment that I won't. But you can take my word for it."

"Let me think through it and I'll get back to you General,"

"Ok, in the meantime I'll let General Garland and Admiral Tyson know about our discussion. They are the only ones who are aware of this. I didn't want to involve any one from your Cabinet for fear of the information leaking."

"That's fine, General," her voice was still shaky, but a measure of composure was returning to her. "I won't take long. A day or two. I know this is urgent, but give me a couple of days."

A quick visit to the rest room to freshen up and then Kate left, looking perfectly composed and in control as far as the rest of the world could tell. But she knew and General Patterson knew the private hell she would have to live through.

CHAPTER 22

*K*ate went home with a heavy heart. She just could not stomach the thought of Hari being a spy. How could he be? Could he have made up all the stuff on religion, philosophy, literature? What about the abiding interest he had shown in her, what she had done before becoming President, how she managed the crisis when they were drifting in the Pacific. Could all that have been just pretense? Was he really capable of such an elaborate, duplicitous plot? She just couldn't bring herself to believe he could. Each time she was about to convince herself that General Patterson was wrong and it was just not possible for Hari to be a spy, her mind would wander to Peter and how he had sprung a surprise out of the blue. If Peter could do it to her after knowing her intimately for seven years, why couldn't Hari do it in twenty one days? And what about her father? He had dumped them all and walked out on them and they had never heard from him again. The men in her life had a pretty abysmal track record. And yet, she could not accept that Hari was a spy who had bold facedly lied to her and deceived her. These same thoughts kept spiraling through her head all night. After tossing around sleeplessly, she finally got out of bed around 6:00 a.m., had a quick shower, and decided to go see Father Duncan. He had come to her rescue so many times in the past year. She would confide in him and seek his advice.

When Kate reached Father Duncan's cottage he was getting ready for breakfast. The unexpected visit from Kate brought a bright smile to his face. "Ah, Kate! So good to see you. Looks like something is bothering you," he said. Her forlorn look and distraught demeanor had told him that all was not well with her. "I was going to have breakfast, come join me," he said and took her by the hand to his spartan dining room.

Over breakfast Kate told him about her relationship with Hari and what General Patterson had told her the previous night about Hari. "Father, I trust General Patterson completely, but my heart tells me Hari is innocent. He is not capable of such a low, despicable thing. What should I do?" she said and her eyes filled up with tears. Father Duncan took her right palm, held it between his hands, and pressed it softly. "Kate, my dear, a well tuned heart is a far more reliable instrument than even the sharpest brain. I would not dismiss your heart's intimations lightly. However, you are no ordinary person. What you do or don't do has great significance to all of us and for the future of this country. So you must tread carefully. For now keep an open mind and try to get more information. This is a very sensitive issue, so you must be careful who you approach for help. I suggest you call President Walters, take him into your confidence and ask for his help. You know you can trust him fully. It should be a pretty simple matter for him to get to the bottom of this. And he will do it very discreetly too."

Kate was relieved. This made perfect sense to her. She took leave of Father Duncan, drove to her office and placed a call to President Walters. President Walters was away for the day, so she wouldn't hear from him until the next day at the earliest. She got busy with the myriad logistical details and policy issues that had piled up, waiting for her attention. Her thoughts kept going back to Hari and the looming disaster, but with great will power she pushed Hari out of her mind each time and returned to her work. The day trudged wearily on. Finally around half past eight at night her exhaustion and lack of sleep caught up with her. She locked up her office, went home, had a shower, ate yogurt for dinner and went to sleep. Mercifully, she fell asleep quickly.

She was woken up early next morning by a call from Henry Winkerman, the Secretary of Law and Order. His voice was shaky and anxious and he was profusely apologetic. "I am very sorry to wake you up so early President Upshaw, but something urgent has come up. I don't want to talk about it over the phone. Can I come by and see you?" He asked.

"Yes. Please come right away. I'll be ready in ten minutes," Kate replied. "What new disaster does today bring?" she thought to herself, as she had a quick shower and got ready.

She got dressed just in time to answer the door for Henry Winkerman. He had a look of nervous embarrassment on his face. "Madame President, I don't quite know how to broach this subject. It has to do with you...," he said and handed her a newspaper. It was an English language newspaper from India. Winkerman had folded the paper so that the front page headlines were clearly visible. The headlines screamed in thick, big capital letters: "IS LOCAL MAN HARI PRESIDENT KATE'S MATE?" Right underneath was a color photo showing Kate in Hari's arms on the Kanyakumari beach. Kate's head was spinning and she lost her balance. Winkerman saw that she was teetering and grabbed her shoulder. "Madame President, are you alright?" he asked walking her towards a chair

192

nearby. "Yes," Kate managed to whisper as she collapsed on to the chair.

"Oh God! Where did you find this?" she asked Winkerman, as soon as she collected herself.

"We get a whole bunch of Indian newspapers every day to monitor what's happening across the border in India. One of my men saw this and brought it over," Winkerman said.

"I don't know what the article says, but what the photo shows is true. I have been seeing this man, Hari," Kate said.

"It's a pretty bad article, Madame President. It makes all kinds of insinuations about you and this man. It claims you are violating the social norms in India and breaking all codes of conduct, setting a bad example for the impressionable youth of India, and causing a great deal of pain and suffering to Hari's orthodox Brahmin parents in their old age. And a lot more."

"The lousy arseholes. They are really exploiting this for all it is worth and then some," Kate said holding her head in her hands.

Winkerman didn't know what the appropriate response was. He waited for a while and said, "Madame President, my deepest sympathies at this outrage. They should let your private life be private. But this paparazzi culture has spread to media all over the world. I want you to know you have my full support. Please tell me, is there anything I can do **to** make this more bearable for you?"

"Thank you Henry. Right now, I need to be able to think things through for myself. I'll call a Cabinet meeting later today and we can discuss this in detail,"

Kate said. Winkerman left, shaking his head in sadness. He liked Kate and was quite deeply affected by this development.

Kate stared at the headlines for a long time. She just couldn't bring herself to read the article. She felt a bitter taste in her mouth, as though she was just recovering from a long bout of illness. She finally forced herself to read the article. The only thing of substance they had was the photograph. The rest of the stuff was just plain nonsense. It traced Hari back to his Southern California days and suggested that he may have known Kate then, since he had lived just a few miles away from her. It talked about Kate's life in Southern California and how she had left her husband to come away on The Nation of Good Hope, and just stopped short of saying that Hari was the main reason for her doing this. To a naïve reader it sounded pretty damning. To any one with even a smattering of knowledge about what had happened on The Nation of Good Hope, it would be immediately obvious that it was made up crap. But even for the latter group, the photograph was pretty shocking. And the cheeky write-up apologizing to the readers for the only photograph on the rock that missed all the action behind the boulder was certainly embarrassing. Kate was fuming, but also partially relieved that it didn't accuse Hari of being a spy trying to get national secrets out of her. "At least that piece is safe for now," she thought, "I must talk to President Walters before this thing blows up."

She asked her assistant to set up an emergency meeting of her Cabinet later in the afternoon. She was hoping President Walters would have called by then and she would have definite information on Hari that she could take with her to the meeting. The thought of facing them made her feel both ashamed and indignant. She felt so helpless. What had she done that was so wrong? Spent some time alone with a smart, hadsome, young Indian. Was that a crime? But didn't she put the country at risk? How could that be when she had told Hari nothing that was sensitive and he had not so much as set foot on The Nation of Good Hope? It was just hypothetical hoopla and a lot of bad optics. But it did raise some questions about the future. If she wanted to take her relationship with Hari somewhere, assuming he was innocent, she would have to sort a lot of things out. She was not sure exactly what the issues were and how they were to be sorted out, but it was clear it would need a lot of thought. But first this thing about Hari being a spy had to be dealt with. If he indeed was a spy, she had no choice, she would have to end it. It was the only option open to her both from a personal and a political point of view. That was clear. There was still a glimmer of hope, though. May be President Walters could help prove Hari's innocence. God! What a difference two days can make in a person's life! Two short days ago she was madly in love and busy defining the policies and laying the foundation for the future of a new country in a new location. She had felt so confident and so sure of herself. And now here she was feeling so unmoored and lost. Both her personal and political life were hanging in a balance. She had no idea how the Cabinet would react. She would be honest and straightforward with them. Tell them that her relationship with Hari was a fact. If President Walters confirmed that Hari was a spy, she would end her relationship with him. If he was proven innocent, then it was her personal matter. She would give her word to the Cabinet and the country that she would safeguard their interests and tell them she would need more time to sort out her relationship with Hari. This was the only honest thing she could do. Seemed amorphous and uncertain, not at all a solid plan befitting a President. But that was the truth. The situation was indeed amorphous and uncertain and would need more time to resolve.

Kate's thoughts were interrupted by a knock on the door. Her assistant entered to tell her that General Patterson was waiting to see her, did she want to see him? Kate was surprised. She wasn't expecting him. "General Patterson? Did he have an appointment?" she asked. "No Mam, he did not. He says he has something he wants to discuss with you urgently," the assistant said. "Alright, send him in," said Kate.

General Patterson walked in. He seemed flushed and excited. Kate stood up to receive him. He walked up to Kate, grasped both her hands and said, "Kate, this is terrible. This slanderous article in the Indian newspaper. Such plain nonsense! They are out to malign and slander you. I am so sorry. I think I have an idea who is behind this."

"General, what do you mean you have an idea who is behind this? This is just some BS being spread by this newspaper to gain cheap publicity."

"I am afraid it is worse than that Kate. I may have been responsible for this."

"What! How could you have anything to do with this? Do you even know these people?"

"No. Here's what happened. I told you I discussed your relationship with Hari with Admiral Tyson and General Garland. We decided we needed to vet it with someone reliable who would be able to verify it for us. General Garland suggested Jack Kent, the CIA Director because CIA has an extensive network in India and it would be easy for them to get all the facts about Hari. Made perfect sense at that time. So I called Jack Kent, told him about your relationship with Hari and asked him to get detailed information about Hari so we could assess if he was a security risk. Two days later he called me back and told me that Hari was a spy with deep connections within the Indian Government and possibly also with foreign defense contractors and was quite likely working for them. It was he who advised me that Hari was a huge security risk and must be stopped right away. That's exactly the message I gave you. And the very next day this Indian newspaper publishes this cheap, trashy story."

"Oh, no! You reached out to Jack Kent. He is a slime ball. We all know how he tried to get President Walters to order the demolition of all the military equipment here. But why would he do this? Why would he want to destroy my life?"

"Kate, you are underestimating Jack Kent, just like all of us did. It has nothing to do with your personal life. He doesn't want the sensitive equipment and the classified defense material to fall into Indian hands. I am sure he knows that we are right now busy figuring out the future of The Nation of Good Hope. The country is here to stay, but not all the people will stay back. That's for sure. In fact, I am not sure about it myself. But the country will be here along with all the sensitive defense stuff. Jack Kent wants to create enough instability and force us to abandon The Nation of Good Hope and return to India. He can then persuade President Walters to have all the defense material shipped back to America. The Indians can take over this territory after that, that wouldn't bother Kent."

"That's diabolical, General. He has no idea what The Nation of Good Hope means to millions of us. Sure, some of the people may go back to America. But the vast majority will stay. I am positive. Father Duncan tells me that too. I am going to be here, no question about that."

"See Kate? That's why he is targeting you. If he makes you lose faith and decide to leave, then most of the rest of the people will follow you. Let's face it. You have been the bedrock for this country. Without you there is no Nation of Good Hope. Kent knows this. It is a clever strategy."

"So you think he leaked this information to the Indian newspaper?"

"I have no proof. But I wasn't born yesterday. The article appeared two days after I talked with him. I don't believe in such coincidences."

"So you think the stuff he said about Hari being a spy may be fake?" Kate asked optimistically.

"Don't know that he would stoop that low. But it is possible. We must get someone to check it out."

"I have a call into President Walters, I'll ask for his help."

"Great idea, Kate. He will do anything to help you. He is one man who can get to the bottom of this quickly. I am sorry I caused so many problems for you."

"Yeah, my life right now is hell. But don't apologize General. I would expect nothing less from you. You were acting out of concern for national security. It was the right thing to do. As for the effects on my personal life, I have to deal with it. That's the price one pays for being in politics I suppose."

General Patterson stayed a little longer to commiserate with Kate on her plight and then left after apologizing again profusely.

Kate got the call from President Walters later in the morning. "Hi Kate! How are you doing? No more motion sickness, huh?" he said. He was in a jovial mood. That changed quickly when Kate told him about her predicament. She was quite open with him. She told him about her involvement with Hari, but stressed that it had been innocuous. They liked each other a lot and longed to meet every day, but that was it. They hadn't discussed any internal issues specific to The Nation of Good Hope. It was all about philosophy, literature, religion, general politics, the travails the Good Hopers had been through, the general state of affairs in India and so on. When she started to tell him about the information General Patterson had given her about Hari possibly being a spy, she couldn't help getting emotional.

"General Patterson did the right thing President Walters, by checking on Hari. He had to do it. Too much was at stake. He went to Jack Kent to have Hari checked out. Jack Kent told him that Hari was a spy who must be stopped at all costs. Right after this the story of my relationship with Hari was leaked to a local Indian newspaper. General Patterson believes the leak came from Jack Kent's people. He thinks Kent is out to destabilize my Government, trying to force us to give up on The Nation of Good Hope and return to America bringing all the defense equipment and classified material with us. That's his only concern. He doesn't give a damn about what we've been through and how we feel," her voice broke.

"Jack can be a bastard, I know. But don't you worry Kate. I know exactly what I need to do get to the bottom of this. With some luck, I should get back to you in the next few hours. You have my word, I'll find out what is going on. And then we can discuss the best course of action for you and everyone else." With that the call ended.

President Walters was quite perturbed. If Kate and General Patterson were right, this was bloody serious. The CIA Director had no authority to initiate covert operations against a foreign government without proper approval. Both the President himself and Congress would have to be consulted and appropriate permissions obtained. He decided to give this matter the highest priority. It was not just critical for Kate, it was vital for him too. He couldn't afford to have a rogue CIA Director on his hands, ignoring the President, the White House and the Congress and acting unilaterally. He made two calls. The first was to the NSA Director. He briefed the NSA Director and told him he wanted a forensic analysis of the photo that appeared in the Indian newspaper and see if they could trace it to a specific camera brand. The next call he made was to the US Ambassador for India in Delhi. The Ambassador already knew about the newspaper article. He gave the Ambassador a quick rundown on his suspicions about Jack Kent and told him to make discreet enquiries about CIA operatives in India, especially in South India. He told the Ambassador he expected NSA to come back to him soon with a report on the photo.

"As soon as I get information about the photo I'll call you myself. This stuff is top priority for me. With that information, you should be able to trace the photo to one of our CIA operatives, if they are indeed involved. And one more thing, find out about this guy Hari. Specifically, I want to know if he has any connections with the Indian Government or any of the defense contractors who operate in India. This is very sensitive. Please be very discreet," he told the Ambassador and hung up.

It didn't take long for NSA to complete its digital forensic analysis. Very early the next morning the NSA Director called President Walters. The camera was a high end Nikon model from the early eighties. Not a common model, a rather pricey one used by professionals with deep pockets who care a lot about image quality and resolution. President Walters immediately called the Indian Ambassador and passed the information along. In a matter of a couple of hours, the Ambassador had the camera traced to a CIA operative based in Madras in Southern India. He also got a report on Hari stating that he had no known connection to the Indian Government, nor was he involved with any defense contractor operating in India. He immediately called President Walters and gave him the full details.

President Walters wasted no time. It was early in the morning, but he didn't care. He summoned Jack Kent to the Oval office. He placed the newspaper article, the NSA forensic analysis, the particulars of the camera and the identity of the CIA operative in Madras to whom it belonged, on the table in front of Jack Kent.

"I am sure you have a perfectly reasonable explanation for this, Jack," he said.

Jack Kent took one look at the evidence in front of him and his face changed color. It had a pale ghostly white hue.

Before he could say anything President Walters said, "And I suppose you also have a perfectly reasonable explanation for the scandalous crap you told General Patterson about that guy Hari." He waited for Jack to answer, but all Kent did was to shuffle his feet uncomfortably and look away. He knew his game was up. He had completely miscalculated. He had not expected General Patterson to tell Kate that he was the person who had given him the dope on Hari. His man in Madras had also been overzealous. He had only asked him to spread some rumors about Kate and Hari, not get a front page article published on it. In his experience, senior military people didn't get so involved with the Government. They preferred to focus on military matters and leave the political intrigue to politicians and civilians. All his years at the CIA had given him excellent training in manipulating a person's emotions, not in understanding the depth of emotions people can have for each other. He had no clue at all how General Patterson felt about Kate.

President Walters delivered the coup de grace swiftly. "I want your resignation by close of business today. Leave now," he said and turned away without shaking hands.

As soon as Kent left, President Walters called Kate. His timing was perfect. Her Cabinet meeting was going to start in half an hour and she could do with some cheering up.

"I have good news for you Kate," President Walters said solemnly as soon as Kate came on the line. "Hari is completely in the clear. Jack Kent not only lied about Hari being a spy, he was also responsible for the newspaper article. One of his CIA operatives took that photo and sent it to the newspaper and pretty much pressured the newspaper into publishing that article. Hari has no connections to the Indian Government or to any defense contractor."

Kate was ecstatic. This was the first encouraging news she had received in two days. "Thank you Mr. President. I'll forever be grateful to you for this. Can I give my Cabinet the full details and can I tell them I got this information directly from you?" she asked.

"I don't see any problem with that. Go ahead and tell them. Just ask them not to let it be known that I was on the phone with you giving you this info. There is nothing sensitive about it. Jack Kent is history. I am looking for a new CIA director right now. I just don't want people talking about the high priority I gave this, that's all."

Kate thanked the President and hung up. She headed for the Cabinet meeting in the best frame of mind she had been in for a long time. It was still a thorny issue to deal with, but it was now a personal matter, not a threat to national security.

Her whole Cabinet had gathered in the conference room. Frank Jewell, the Secretary of Defense, Dr. Kirk Sanders, the Secretary of Science and Technology, Sam Turnbull, the Secretary of Civil Supplies, Henry Winkerman the Law and Order Secretary, they all sat looking pretty glum. They had all seen the newspaper article about Kate and Hari by now. But such was the high esteem in which they held Kate that instead of indulging in the customary gossip on so inviting a topic, they sat in silence waiting for her. The three military leaders were there too. Kate had asked them to be there, since issues pertaining to national security were expected to be discussed.

Kate was completely honest and forthright with them. She started out by admitting she was in a relationship with Hari, she had been seeing him for three weeks. They hadn't had the time to work out all the logistical details, but they had committed to be together. They had to figure out how to make it happen and that would take time. The future of The Nation of Good Hope, its relationship to India and America in particular, and to the rest of the world, had to become clearer before she could plan her life with Hari.

"I am confident that I can deal with this situation and do what's best for The Nation of Good Hope and me. However, if you as a group doubt my ability to do that, I am willing to resign. The country needs strong leadership now at this critical stage and I don't want to become a liability. I love this country far too much for that," her eyes teared up. Frank Jewell and the military leaders were relatively impassive, but the rest of them had clearly become emotional. "And one more thing. There is another issue that most of you with the exception of General Patterson, General Garland and Admiral Tyson, are unaware of. General Patterson had received information that Hari was a spy trying to trap me with the hope of gaining access to our military secrets," she paused. There was an audible gasp from several people, including Frank Jewell. Only the military leaders remained unmoved. "I just got off the phone with President Walters, before I came over here. I have it directly from him that Hari was falsely accused. He is completely innocent. It was an elaborate ruse form Jack Kent, the CIA Director, to destabilize our country. His aim was to persuade us to abandon The Nation of Good Hope and return to America. This was his way of ensuring that the military equipment and classified defense material we have here remains within America." Kate went on to give them the full details of everything she had learnt from President Walters. When she was done, General Patterson stood up. He was beaming. He walked to Kate, shook her hand and said, "I am so relieved to hear this President Upshaw. I couldn't be happier for you." The whole room broke into a loud applause. They all gathered around her, congratulating her and shaking hands. The crisis had passed, though Kate still had the main issue unresolved. The task of planning her life with Hari was far from simple. It most definitely would need more time. At least another year or so.

CHAPTER 23

*H*ari hadn't seen or heard from Kate for four days now. There was no question of hearing, they had to meet in person to communicate. There was no other way. And Kate hadn't come by. He had been in a terrible state of mind since that morning when the newspaper article had appeared. He had been shocked, not so much by the fact that their relationship had become public – that didn't particularly bother him – but by the slanderous insinuations the article made. The suggestion that he might have had a relationship with Kate back in LA in the nineties, even when she was married to Peter, was particularly hurtful to him. What he found equally galling was the moralizing the article indulged in, saying what a bad influence this would be on the Indian youth and how society had to curb such acts. The claims made about how shattered his aged parents would be, especially his mother, had affected him a lot. Because this, indeed, was true. His parents would most definitely be upset. He was sure he could explain it to them, make them understand, even accept it. He had a very close relationship with both his parents and loved them deeply, so he was confident he could get them to come to terms with it. He had been sufficiently detached from the local community that he didn't really care what they thought of him. He had the reputation of being a weird guy who kept to himself, any way, so that aspect of it didn't bother him at all. He knew this would be devastating for Kate so he wanted desperately to meet her, talk to her, console her, reassure her that they would emerge from this mess stronger. In fact, he would have liked to start making plans for their future together right then and there, but he knew that was impossible. There were just too many unresolved issues Kate had to iron out first. If Kate continued to be President, then she couldn't possibly live in India. And if he had to move to The Nation of Good Hope, they would have to have broad policies in place for dealing with foreigners. It was certainly premature to start planning their lives together. How were they supposed to deal with this meretricious gossip, then? He needed to talk it over with Kate.

Hari waited for Kate patiently on their rock. He knew it was not very likely that she would come to see him that day. That article would have caused such a ruckus over there. She would be more than busy trying to deal with the after effects. "Poor girl, she must be going crazy," he thought, "how I wish I were with her. At least we could talk things over and strategize." Thinking about Kate made him more agitated. He had the luxury of sitting here by himself to brood and feel sorry. She must be going crazy there, desperate to see him and talk to him. Instead, she had to deal with this scandal, explain it to the people. "How the hell is she coping?" he thought. After spending a few hours on the rock, tortured, his thoughts in a whirlwind, he decided to go into town and spend some time with his parents. At least he could deal with his side of the story.

As soon as his mother saw him, she came rushing to him, hugged him and said in a rebuking tone in Tamil, "What's all this son? What have you done? And is what they are saying true, that you knew her back in America and that's why she came here. Because you are here," she spoke breathlessly. She was in tears.

"Amma," Hari said, "yes, I love Kate. But no, I didn't know her in America. Never saw her or heard of her. Just happened to meet her on the beach three weeks ago after they landed up next to us. Don't believe everything you read in that rag. You know what crap they write."

That didn't calm his mother. "What's all this love nonsense? Is this why you refused to get married all these years? No local girl was good enough for you? I showed you photos of so many pretty girls from our own caste, but you rejected them all. Why? Because you were waiting for this woman?" she said.

Hari was pretty cool. His mother was an open book to him. He knew what her reaction was going to be. He could have almost predicted her exact words. "Amma, you are getting emotional and carried away. I don't have to answer your accusations, you know none of it is true. You know very well what kind of a guy I am. I am fussy with some things, I was waiting for the right girl, that's all. I didn't know she would come floating over the ocean to me. But she did. Don't you see? This is Kanyakumari returning to Shiva. I am her Shiva and she is my Kanyakumari."

His mother was stunned. Hari had made the reference to Kanyakumari and Shiva on an impulse, without thinking, but it stirred her to the depth of her soul. She was a deeply religious, God fearing woman. She fully believed the legend of Kanyakumari. She went to the temple every Friday to do Puja. Hari's words created a thrilling, electrifying wave in her. She turned to her husband who had been observing this drama silently and asked, "Did you hear what Hari said? Do you believe it?"

"It is possible. God's ways are strange and mysterious. Who are we to say what should or shouldn't happen?" he said philosophically. The atmosphere in the house changed in an instant. Hari's mother rushed to the Puja room and stood in silent prayer for a long time, her hands folded. She finally emerged and facing Hari, asked, "When am I going to see Kumari?"

It took Hari a minute to grasp what she was saying. "Kumari? Oh…,you mean Kate…." His mother interrupted him, "Don't call her Kate. She is Kumari. We are Vishnu worshippers, that's why we named you Hari, but from today you are also Shiva for me. I am not going to change your name, but that's what you are," she said. Hari was another name for Lord Vishnu who along with Shiva and Brahma formed the famed Indian Trinity.

So that was that. With the recasting of Kate as Kanyakumari, her acceptance within Hari's family was complete. Hari's mother was the key influencer in the family and his father simply followed her lead. They had many excited discussions through the day about the next steps. When would the marriage take place, where would they live, and much more. His mother even wondered aloud what the kids would look like. "She is very pretty, so the kids will look good," she said feeling proud. Hari left at the end of the day feeling partially happy that at least his side of the story had been settled. Kate's would be a far bigger challenge, he knew. They would just have to wait and see how things developed.

CHAPTER 24

*K*ate was restless. Her relationship with Hari becoming public was weighing heavily on her. Even though the cabinet had supported her, she could sense an undercurrent of unrest among them. And who could blame them? They had all been through so much and there were still so many unknowns and uncertainties to negotiate. What was the future of the nation of Good Hope? Could it remain a separate entity without being gobbled up by India? As long as President Walters was at the helm he would ensure that. He would park the US Seventh Fleet right there in the Indian Ocean, if necessary. But what about the longer term? In ten years would America have the same interest in The Nation of Good Hope as they did today? Right now the vast majority of Americans thought of the Good Hopers as Americans and there was great sympathy and support for them. That was the main reason President Walters had been able to get Congress to approve over a hundred billion dollars in aid for The Nation of Good Hope. A cash grant with no strings attached. In a few years Americans were bound to lose interest in them. That was certain. What would happen then? Would India leave them alone? What about China? Would they start evincing undue interest in them? Who could tell? These were unanswerable questions. Much depended on what she and her government did in the next few years. If they could emulate Singapore and become an economic powerhouse while maintaining a stable government and a happy, contended population, they had a great chance of continuing to be free and independent.

The British had walked out of Singapore virtually overnight after the second world war, leaving the country with nothing, no money, no food, no infrastructure and still reeling from the ravages of war. Out of desperation, the make shift bunch of leaders had negotiated a merger with Malaysia which only lasted for a short time. The Malaysians saw no advantage in being burdened with a ragtag bunch of people from a poor island with no resources. Under the leadership of Lee Kuan Yew, Singapore had broken from Malaysia and become a separate country again. With gargantuan effort, iron will, and military discipline, Yew who became the first Prime Minister of Singapore, had forged a highly successful, modern state. That would be the model for Kate. She would have to emulate Prime Minister Yew without employing the authoritarian tactics he had resorted to. That was no way an option for her. The Good Hopers, reared on capitalistic democracy in America, would not stand for it. Kate knew this. She was clear on the end result she needed to achieve. The path to get there was far from clear. And this scandal made things that much harder. By now practically everyone on The Nation of Good Hope had heard about her and Hari. It had been a constant discussion topic on all TV channels. There were lots of speculations about what would happen next. Would Kate marry Hari? If so, when? Would Hari come to live with her? What would his status be? Would Hari having such a prominent role be a temptation to other Indians? Would they try to sneak their way in? What would The Nation of Good Hope have to do to ensure its sovereignty and independence? The country was rife with gossip and rumors.

Kate decided it was time to put an end to all the speculation. That very night she appeared on TV and addressed the country and leveled with them, just as she

211

had done with her Cabinet. She admitted frankly and honestly that she was in love with Hari. She assured the people that her immediate priority was not Hari. In fact she had not seen him or talked to him since all this became public. She had no time. She would devote all her energy to figuring out the next steps for The Nation of Good Hope. She would work with the Cabinet to address the immediate, pressing issues; security, food, water, energy, guiding the country back to being a free market economy, distribution of the aid money from America to get everyone back on their feet, a myriad issues. Only when she and her Cabinet felt they had a firm grip on all these issues would she start planning her life with Hari. She would of course want to keep seeing Hari in the meantime. She would talk to her Cabinet about a proper mechanism for allowing Hari unrestricted visitor's privileges. A sort of temporary passport that would give him unrestricted entry to The Nation of Good Hope with the ability to stay for several weeks at a time. She explained all this to the people calmly and rationally and appealed to them for their cooperation and support.

The response was overwhelming. The people had seen her performance during the yearlong crisis. They had no reason to doubt her. She was an attractive, young, woman who needed a man in her life. Yeah, it would have been better if it were a Good Hoper. But a smart, spirited, extremely capable young woman should be allowed to pursue her love, they owed it to her. This was what the people had felt. And the Cabinet had gone along with it.

The Cabinet and the military leaders had come to her saying it would be good to hold a national referendum to let people decide whether they wanted to stay there or return to America. They agreed to hold a referendum in six months. That would give them time to make arrangements for the several million people who were expected to choose to leave. They would have to build runways and harbors and discus with the American Government the logistical details of transporting such a large number of people back to America. They would figure these details out in the next six months.

The Cabinet supported issuing a special passport to Hari. General Patterson authorized a temporary permit to allow Hari to come and go as he liked and stay up to 4 weeks at a time within The Nation of Good Hope.

On the fourth day after the newspaper leak, Kate went to meet Hari. She had told General Patterson she would be going and he had told her that from then on she would go with a proper escort who would be instructed to respect her privacy. He had sent an MP ahead of time to alert Hari that Kate was coming. Hari was thrilled beyond words. The two hours he had to wait in his cottage before Kate got there were excruciating. Finally Kate arrived, escorted by four MPs. She knocked on the door and ran into his arms hugging him and kissing him.

"Kate! They can see. They are looking," Hari said feeling embarrassed.

"I don't care! They should expect this. They all know about us," Kate Said.

The MPs broke into an involuntary applause and cheered them on shouting "Yeah!". Kate waved to them and walked in telling them over her shoulder that she would be in there for two hours. Hari waved to the MPs pleasantly and closed the door.

They had not quite realized it, but both Hari and Kate had tears streaming down their cheeks. They hugged again and kissed passionately. Kate pulled away, reached into her purse, pulled out a small box neatly gift wrapped and gave it to Hari saying "Here is your gift for being a good boy and waiting patiently."

"Wow! A gift for me! Don't tell me you are proposing!" Hari exclaimed.

He took the box, opened it eagerly and took out a small booklet with a hard cover. On the cover it said Temporary Passport of The Nation of Good Hope. Inside was the signed authorization from General Patterson giving Hari unlimited access to The Nation of Good Hope. Hari quickly glanced at it.

"A passport! Darling Kate! How did you manage this?" he hugged her and kissed her.

Kate told him all that had transpired in the last few days, starting with the startling accusation of Hari being a spy and ending with the vindication from President Walters, her address to the people, the overwhelming support she had received from them, the Cabinet standing by her and giving its approval for issuing Hari a temporary passport.

"I have promised them that for the next six months you will be my second priority," she said.

"Are you kidding? Why six months, I am ready to wait six years if that is what it takes."

He had a pretty good idea of the logistical challenges ahead of her. "Tell me what I can do to help, let's focus our combined energies and do our best to set The Nation of Good hope on a stable path."

"Thanks Hari. But…" said Kate hesitantly, "we have to be very careful how we approach this. Remember, you are a foreigner to everyone except me. They will definitely view you with more than a little suspicion. They are very wary of India, you know. They don't want to be swallowed wholesale by this gigantic country with its one billion people. There is genuine concern and apprehension there. So we have to move very slowly and carefully. You should have no official role at all. At least in the beginning. I will introduce you to Father Duncan. You will have so much to discuss with him, Nilima, and the rest of Father Duncan's helpers. No one has the pulse of the Good Hopers like Father Duncan. He will know what to do, how to get the Good Hopers to know you and trust you."

"I understand, Kate. You are absolutely right. We can't look at this just from within our bubble. The average citizen in The Nation of Good Hope must have his head full to bursting with concerns. You and I can't be adding to that. I agree with you. We must tread very carefully. I want to meet father Duncan. From everything you have told me, he seems like such a great person to get to know."

"Come at 5:00 p.m. tomorrow, Hari. I'll have an MP come pick you up. Come to my office first and then we can go meet Father Duncan," Kate said. It was getting late for her. They hugged and kissed one last time and then Kate left.

The next evening when Hari went to Kate's office he caused a big stir. As soon as the MP escorted him into the building, he was recognized and surrounded by the office

215

staff. They all wanted to say Hi and chat. Word spread that Hari was in the building and everyone left their desks and came running to the lobby. There was an electric air of excitement, as though a rock star had landed unexpectedly. The younger women, in particular, were screaming loudly and quite unprofessionally. The MP was flabbergasted. Hari took it all in his stride, it didn't bother him or overwhelm him in the least. Even he was surprised at how calm he was. He just stood there smiling at everybody affably and exchanged pleasantries. Women at the back couldn't wait to meet him. They were desperately trying to weave their way through the crowd of forty or fifty people who had gathered. There were already side discussions going. You could hear bits and pieces of conversations. "He's so handsome!" "No wonder she fell for him!" "I wonder how they met?" "I want to ask him if he has a brother." At least for now, Hari, the foreigner, had been replaced by Hari, the romantic figure. Whatever concerns they might have felt when Kate addressed them and told them about her relationship with a foreigner, had vanished from their minds. The sheer romance of it all had grabbed the crowd's attention and fears of national security had been cast aside.

Hari made his way to Kate's office. The crowd followed him. Kate heard the commotion and came out. She saw the crowd in front of her office and was taken aback for a second. She quickly regained her poise, took Hari's arm, and facing the crowd said, "I guess you've all met him already. This is Hari, my, my,…," she hesitated, not quite sure what to say. "Friend, very good friend," Hari stepped in grinning. "At least that's what we'll be for the next six months to a year, until things settle down here." The crowd roared in approval and clapped. Kate took him by the hand and tried to get back into her office. "Speech! Speech! Speech!" the crowd shouted. Kate came back out and stood facing the crowd holding Hari's hand. "What can I say," she said, "I've already told you everything in my national address." "We want a speech from Hari," someone shouted. "Oh, Ok," she said and turned to Hari. He didn't appear in the least to be affected by the exuberant reaction from the crowd. He stood there smiling pleasantly and the crowd kept shouting "Speech! Speech! Speech!"

Hari waved to the crowd and still smiling started to speak. "Friends, it is such a pleasure to be here and meet you all. I just can't get over this. I was a part of you seven years ago. I used to live near Laguna Beach." "Yeah!" yelled someone who probably had lived somewhere around Laguna beach before the disaster struck. Hari continued, "I may have even seen some of you in coffee shops, restaurants, malls, or beaches around LA. We may even have been stuck in the same traffic jam. I lived there for almost five years, you know. Which means I must have spent at least six months in traffic jams," he laughed. The crowd laughed approvingly. They hadn't forgotten the infamous LA traffic jams. "So I am not quite sure what I am doing right now. Am I coming to your homeland? Or have you come to mine? Or are we both home where we belong?" The crowd roared again. They were loving it. "In any case," Hari continued, "I'll be coming here very often, so you'll get to see me quite a bit. I hope to meet you all and get to know you," he said and waved. The crowd roared again. Kate and Hari then went into her office. People stood around for a while talking and slowly they dispersed. "That was quite a performance," said Kate. "You are a pro."

They didn't know it at that time, but somehow a KLAN reporter had got wind of Hari coming to Kate's office. He had arrived there with his cameraman just in time to catch Kate and Hari talking. The video clip played again and again that evening on KLAN and its affiliates all over The Nation of Good Hope. Pretty soon it had made its way to all the channels in America, and within hours to the rest of the world. It went viral and caused a huge sensation worldwide. It was nothing short of tumultuous in India. Every Indian channel, local, regional, or national, broadcast the video clip, with local language subtitles, repeating it many times. Kate was already well known, now Hari too became world famous. Particularly so in The Nation of Good Hope, America, and India.

The interaction with the crowd had taken up a lot of time, so Kate had to rush to Father Duncan's cottage. She wanted Hari to spend at least an hour with him before Father Duncan had to leave for his evening program. They reached the cottage just before 6:00 p.m. He was expecting them. He beamed at Kate and shook hands with Hari warmly. "Welcome, Hari, my son," he said. Hari replied, "It is such a pleasure to meet you Father Duncan. I've heard so much about you from Kate in the past few weeks that I feel like I've known you all my life."

"Kate tells me you are very much into philosophy, literature and religion," Father Duncan said. "I don't know much about literature, but on the other two subjects I have done some studying and reflecting. I look forward to having some in-depth discussions with you." Turning to Kate he added, "Kate, what are your plans for the evening? Are you free to join us for dinner?"

Kate replied, "Sorry Father, my evening is packed with back to back meetings. I was planning to spend a half hour here with you and drop Hari back in my office so the MP could escort him back." "In that case Kate, do you mind if Hari stays with me here? He can have dinner with me and then come with me to the TV studio to watch the show. He can come back to my cottage after the show, I would like to chat with him for awhile. After that the MP can pick him up from here and take him back. Is that alright?" "That is perfect, Father. Assuming Hari is fine with that," Kate said. "Of course," Hari said, "I would love to spend time with Father Duncan." Kate spent some more time talking to Father Duncan and Hari, and then headed back to her office, leaving instructions for the MP to meet Hari at Father Duncan's cottage at 11:00 p.m. to take him back to Kanyakumari.

Hari had dinner with Father Duncan. Over dinner Father Duncan asked Hari about his background. He did not know anything about Hari. Kate, of course, had not mentioned Hari before that day. He did hear about the newspaper article, but had refrained from reading it as he made a point of not reading or listening to deliberately slanderous material, if he could avoid it. All he knew was that Hari used to live in the US and had come back to India several years ago. Hari told him that he used to live in Southern California and left after the 1992 Gulf Storm war out of sheer disgust. Hari described how he had spent these last few years in India reading philosophy, religion and literature. The more he listened, the more impressed Father Duncan became with Hari.

After dinner they drove to the T.V. studio with Nilima and two other women. Hari watched from outside while Father Duncan and others went on stage for their show. Nilima and her friends sang several beautiful Bhagavad Gita verses in Sanskrit and then explained their meaning in English. After they finished singing, Father Duncan talked for about thirty minutes giving his interpretation of the message the verses were conveying. He drew parallels from the Bible frequently to convey the hidden meaning of unfamiliar metaphors so his largely Christian audience could better appreciate the intent of the Gita verses. Hari was really impressed. He had never heard or read anything like this before. The verses dealt with a deep psychoanalysis of the human mind and talked about how excessive attachment to sense objects causes anger, frustration and loss of wisdom, and leads to complete destruction. He was quite familiar with the Sanskrit verses and their meaning. He was unaware of any comparable analysis in any western religious literature. But Father Duncan had no difficulty in quoting from the Bible to draw parallels and explain the verses. After the show was over, Hari told Father Duncan and Nilima how much he had enjoyed it. "I know the Gita quite well and still I found the show really informative," Hari said.

Father Duncan dropped Nilima and the other women at their apartments and he and Hari drove back to the cottage. Father Duncan made some tea and both of them made themselves comfortable in the study and settled down to a discussion.

"Tell me Hari," Father Duncan started, "I am rather new to Hinduism. What I find really appealing is how it combines deep abstraction only suited for advanced philosophical discourses, with simple devotion. A learned philosopher can debate what is meant by Aham Brahmasmi, I am God, while a common villager can worship a stone idol. Both are equally permissible. I find this pretty unique, I don't see this in any other religion."

"Father Duncan," Hari replied, "I am not a scholar of Hinduism or philosophy. I am interested in both, so I have done some studying and spent time discussing with some great Swamijis. This is my understanding of the thought process that gave rise to Hinduism as we know it today. Many millennia ago our sages realized through deep meditation that the purpose of human life is to seek God. Not just the Swamis, monks, philosophers; every single human being had to seek God. There was no escaping it, every single person had to do it in whatever limited form. This was the only purpose of life. This is a pretty profound realization.

"They knew from their own experience that it was a very hard, daunting, task fraught with many missteps and distractions. So they thought man needs guidance to help him in his search for God. Now, how does one provide guidance when most people are not even conscious of the fact that they are seeking God? Some kind of crude pagan worship has always existed throughout human history. But that is worship of God arising from the fear of the unknown, not a heartfelt seeking after God. The ancient Indian sages exalted this pagan worship into a religious seeking in the form of Hinduism. Being great intellects and seers, the sages intuited the notion of Aham Bhramasmi, I am God. God is in everything and everything is in God. But, this is a highly abstract concept. With all the evidence from Quantum Physics, we are still struggling to grasp this notion. How was a layman to understand this and contemplate deeply upon on it and be guided by it? So they came up with this brilliant line of thinking. Since God is in everything, why don't we encourage people to see God in whatever they want. A tree, or a rock formation, or whatever pagan idol they were worshipping. So they said worship whatever you want whole heartedly, with all the devotion you can summon, and you will be on the right path. This simple message aided by great mythological stories such as Ramayana, made its way deeply into the consciousness of the Indian people. This is what led to the polymorphic - many gods – aspect of Hinduism, which in its true essence is monotheistic in a deeper sense than any other religion. It proclaims there is only one God. Jesus Christ, Shiva, Vishnu, call him what you want, there is only one of Him. His manifestations are infinite. All of nature, the whole wide cosmos, is God manifest."

"To the western mind raised on Christianity, the notion of idol worship appears to be so primitive and stupid, and yet it is so deep. Incredible, something so profound gets brushed aside as the inane, mindless act of a crude, uncivilized people. Who are the uncivilized people here?" Father Duncan remarked. "People all over the world must understand this beautiful concept."

Hari was inspired. Father Duncan's interest had stirred what was a deep passion within him. "You are right, Father. People all over the world are clamoring for the same thing. Whether they are laymen, scientists, Hindus, Christians, Jews, Muslims, whatever they are. This search for God transcends everything else. All five billion of us are in pursuit of one single thing – God. This is what the Indian sages realized.

"Religion must be all encompassing, it must explain the whole universe, not just some tiny part of it. God either made all of it, or none of it. And religion must be accessible to every human being, from the deepest intellectual to the humblest rural peasant. Religion must be God centered, but circular. At one end it needs to be deep and abstract, and at the other end it must be touchy, feely, plainly palpable. The two ends must loop back on themselves and meet in a full circle. That is where high abstraction meets coarse reality. Aham Brahmasmi meets idol worship. This is what Hinduism is all about."

"Remarkable," Father Duncan said, "I had never understood it this way."

"So our sages said, invoke God into whatever object you like – a tree, a rock, the charming image of Krishna, whatever you like. And worship that object with devotion, and you will be seeking God earnestly," Hari continued, repeating himself. But he wanted to say something more. "The ritual worship we see in Hindu homes and temples is a more formalized version of this concept. Even the architecture of Hindu temples reflects this philosophy. When you enter a temple, you typically go through a series of chambers, each progressively darker, until you finally reach the inner sanctum where the image of God is kept. This symbolizes the progressive stages of withdrawal from the world around and the interiorization of the mind you must achieve, before you can focus and visualize God. The tall Gopuram above the sanctum – which looks like a church steeple – represents the lofty height to which you must raise your consciousness to truly seek God. This is the goal of Yoga, to help you achieve the interiorization of the mind and the raising of your consciousness. And the Aarti, the lighting of the holy lamp, showing the image of God in its light, symbolizes the cosmic light one sees if one raises his consciousness suitably."

"How profound and beautiful!" Father Duncan exclaimed, "I am truly learning something deep. It touches your heart and your mind. Quite eye opening."

"The sad part, Father," Hari continued, "is that hardly a handful of Indians are aware of this. They visit the temple blindly, more out of a sense of obligation. They are totally clueless about what it represents and what they are supposed to be feeling. Even most of the pujaris – the temple priests

– don't know these things. But still, even this blind faith provides a bedrock that is the true strength of India."

Father Duncan was impressed beyond words. "Hari," he said, "our people here need to understand this, how profound Indian spirituality is. Can you help us? Are you willing? Do you have the time?"

"Of course Father, I will. What do you want me to do?"

"Let me think about the best way to present this to our people. Can you come back tomorrow morning? I will give it some thought in the meantime and we can discuss more."

It was already quite late in the night. Father Duncan sent Hari off, accompanied by the MP. Hari returned to his cottage in a happy frame of mind. All the mental agitation he had suffered in the past few days was gone, replaced by feelings of anticipation and excitement.

By the time Hari returned the next morning, Father Duncan had a plan. He would make Hari a part of his evening T.V. show. The last fifteen minutes of the show would be devoted to a discussion between Father Duncan and Hari on Indian spirituality. The aim was to peel the onion for the T.V. audience and show them the many layers of thought embodied in Hinduism and, more generally, in Hindu culture and its way of life.

CHAPTER 25

*T*he issue with Hari having been sorted out, Kate now threw her full energy into addressing the problems confronting The Nation of Good Hope. When it was a part of Southern California, the land area that became The Nation of Good Hope had been quite self sufficient in terms of food. For fresh water and electricity, it had relied critically on Northern California. With the fresh water supply from rivers, streams and lakes having reduced to a trickle after the separation, they were in dire need of new fresh water sources. Lack of fresh water had severely affected agriculture, drastically impacting the growth of fruits and vegetables that Southern California had been so renowned for. Reserves of electricity were extremely low, and if they had to revive the economy and industry and reach anything like their old levels, they would need to figure out alternative sources of power. Kate had had several discussions with President Walters about getting American assistance for building a large nuclear plant that would make them completely self sufficient in terms of their power needs. They were also relying on American assistance to build a large desalination plant that could generate enough fresh water for their needs. They never could produce enough fresh water to go back to the kind of irrigation based agriculture that had existed before. They would have to import all their fresh foods from India and the surrounding countries for the time being until they had a better handle on how their soil would adapt to the new weather conditions and rainfall patterns. President Walters had instructed his administration to look into alternatives for building a nuclear plant and a desalination plant in The Nation of Good Hope. They had assembled a team of experts who were waiting for final reports on the seismological stability of The Nation of Good Hope before coming over to start exploring options for a nuclear plant and a desalination plant. Natural gas was not a problem, they had large supplies of that.

Sam Turnbull, the Secretary of Civil Supplies, had been busy working with the U.S. Agriculture Secretary to figure out the details of food items that could be obtained from America and what they should import from other countries. All the wheat, corn and frozen meat they needed would be supplied by America. Fresh food, dairy, poultry, rice, beans and other items would have to be imported from India and other surrounding countries. The U.S. Agriculture Secretary also advised Sam Turnbull to negotiate with India to obtain a supply of fresh water and electricity to meet their needs for the near future.

Kate had already begun discussions with President Walters and Prime Minister Dalal to plan for the evacuation of the several million Americans who were expected to go back to America. They would need several new runways to be built. President Walters had ordered the latest American technology to be made available to construct the runways in record time. General Paterson had identified about ninety relatively safe docking points for ships to transport people by sea. They had begun the process of assembling the largest peacetime collection of ships. President Walters had put Admiral Roland in charge of coordinating the sea-evacuation again.

The international team of experts had arrived, as promised by President Walters, to determine the stability of the landmass. Two weeks of extensive undersea experiments had confirmed that the landmass had settled firmly on the ocean floor for the most part. Only deep into the ocean, some twenty miles into the water, a significant gap separated the bottom of the landmass from the ocean floor. Practically all the experts had agreed that this posed no threat to the stability of the landmass. The vulnerability to changes in surface pressure distribution was gone. There was still the question of long term instability due to possible undersea erosion, but that could wait. People were now free to move about as they liked. Schools were reopened and school buses began to ply their familiar routes again.

The team of experts had brought in sophisticated undersea drilling equipment to test for any leftover gas trapped deep in subterranean chambers. They had drilled deep into the side of the crust all around the landmass. There had been no sign of gas. Emboldened by this, the team had drilled trough many points on the surface as well. They had not found any gas, except for the known deposits of natural gas closer to the surface that had historically met the needs of Southern California. The jet stream activity had completely vanished. The rocketship no longer existed. It had disappeared without a trace. Quite incredibly, everything had fallen into place. The seismological phenomenon was history. The false calm that seemed to exist on the surface of the landmass when the jet stream was in full flow had been replaced by a real calmness arising out of the even more incredible phenomenon of cultural, behavioral and spiritual metamorphosis.

Kate and her Cabinet had flown to Delhi to meet Prime Minister Dalal and his Cabinet. The meetings were to discuss the needs of The Nation of Good Hope and how

India could help them. They needed Indian assistance in multiple areas. Food, electricity, fresh water, all had to be imported from India for the foreseeable future. Prime Minister Dalal and Kate agreed to form a joint committee to figure out how best India could help The Nation of Good Hope in these areas. They also agreed to work jointly to determine the best options to build roads and bridges to connect The Nation of Good Hope to India. They agreed to work together to establish appropriate immigration and customs mechanisms to facilitate movement of people and goods. A new fiber optic cable was going to be laid to connect The Nation of Good Hope to Madras, to enable easy communication between the two countries.

Kate had created new Cabinet positions to come up with policies to guide the economy, global trade and foreign affairs, including immigration. Stimulating the economy and industry and transitioning to a market economy was a very tricky proposition. They had to figure out what kind of an economic and social model they should aim for. Immigration, passport and visa policies had to be defined. This too was a tricky proposition given that they were surrounded by over populated Asian countries. Reasonable border control polices had to be defined to regulate the flow of people across the border with India. Trade and commerce were relatively simple matters. They had plenty of cash and there were surrounded by many countries eager to do business. Every day Kate met with delegations from surrounding countries proposing trade agreements. They had to come up with a general framework such as the NAFTA which had governed all the commercial activities between the U.S., Canada and Mexico. These preoccupations consumed a large part of Kate's time. She found it both exhausting and exhilarating at the same time.

Father Duncan, Hari and Nilima had had a deep impact on the people. Father Duncan's evening T.V. program had expanded to two hours, from 7:30 p.m. to 9:30 p.m. It now included a children's program from 7:30 p.m. to 8:00 p.m. The children's program focused on exposing the kids to Indian mythological stories from the classics, The Ramayana and Mahabharata, and tales of wisdom from the Panchatantra. The adults' program created a unique blend of preachings and sermons from the Bible and recitations and interpretations from the Vedas and the Bhagavad Gita. The focus was on showing how the two rich religious traditions had approached very similar subjects from very different perspectives, leading to the same conclusions and end results. Father Duncan, Hari and Nilima had woven an extraordinary cross-cultural, inter-religious, fabric warm enough to melt the coldest of hearts. They had created a perfect spiritual blend of the East and the West and the people had responded overwhelmingly. It was small wonder, then, that when General Patterson conducted the promised referendum to determine how many people wanted to leave The Nation of Good Hope and go back to America, less than two million people elected to leave. About six million opted to stay back and the remaining four million or so were undecided; they were in a quandary, unable to decide. The prevailing feeling among the people was that they were brought here for a purpose and it would be wrong to leave in defiance. And yet, the sheer mystery and foreignness of India caused a great deal of concern and apprehension among the people. A lot of people would need help in making their choice. People were already coming to Father Duncan asking for his advice.

Hari had become a regular fixture on The Nation of Good Hope. Every morning an MP would pick him up and bring him over to The Nation of Good Hope. He spent all day with Father Duncan, Nilima and the rest of the people who assisted Father Duncan in running The Church of Good Hope. Much of his time went in preparing for the day's T.V. show and helping Father Duncan with various administrative issues. An MP would take him back at night after the T.V. show. Sometimes he would get into some deep discussion with Father Duncan until very late in the night. On such occasions, Father Duncan would insist that he spend the night there. Kate was much too busy to join them regularly. She would come over once in a while and spend some time with them. More often, Hari would go over to her office when she had some free time and they would have lunch and go for a walk on the beach, or just sit somewhere and talk. They didn't feel any anxiety about their plans for the future. They had both accepted that it would take a while to iron out the wrinkles and set The Nation of Good Hope on the best path forward. It simply couldn't be rushed and there was no point in getting worked up about it. A comfortable routine had developed and both Hari and Kate were content.

Hari's mother was getting more and more restless and impatient that Hari was not getting married. She had expected them to get married in a few weeks. Several months had gone by now and there was still no sign of marriage. She confronted Hari once and asked him, "Son, what is taking so long? Why are you delaying? You keep telling me she is too busy. If she is too busy to get married, then how will she ever have time to be a wife or a mother?" Hari could not make her understand all the transition issues Kate had to deal with and why it was not a good idea for them to get married before those issues had been settled. Exasperated, his mother had told him, "I am getting old and feeble, I don't think I will live to see your marriage. Can I at least see Kumari? Can you bring her home?" Hari didn't have the heart to say no to her. He talked to Kate about it. Kate agreed, though she was apprehensive about it.

On a Sunday evening he sneaked Kate into his house after dark. Instead of the usual Military Police van, he had arranged for an Indian car to pick Kate up so that they would not attract attention. When Hari took Kate, dressed in a plain green sari, looking lovelier and more elegant than ever, to his parents' house, his mother had embraced Kate. She had performed the traditional *Aarti*, the ceremonial welcome with the lamps, before allowing her in. That had assured Hari that Kate had been accepted, there would be no problem. His mother, who spoke no English, had simply held Kate's chin softly and looked into her eyes. Hari's father had conversed with Kate in his broken English and tried his best to make her feel at home. Kate and Hari had to cut their dinner short and rush back because the news of Kate's presence there spread despite their best efforts to keep it a secret and a crowd began gathering in front of their house. Worried that there could be security issues and undesirable press coverage, they had bid hasty goodbyes and rushed back.

The visit left a lasting and confusing impression on Kate. Driving into the heart of Kanyakumari, even in the darkness she could feel how foreign and different that ancient land was. It was like nothing she had experienced before. The place was teeming with people. The streets, shops, houses, everything looked different. It was strangely peaceful and chaotic at the same time. And her experience inside Hari's house was both baffling and heartwarming. She had liked Hari's parents a lot, even though she had not said much to them. She had felt their affection for her, and she had responded by touch, gesture and looks more than with words, to convey her emotions.

231

CHAPTER 26

*T*he stream of people seeking advice from Father Duncan was growing every day, to the point where he could no longer cope with it. Talking this over with Hari, Father Duncan decided to convert a portion of the church into an Office of Community Services and put Hari and Nilima in charge. Their main job was to meet the constant throng of people coming with concerns and anxieties about what staying back on The Nation of Good Hope would entail, what their future would be like, could they enjoy the same life they had before the disaster, how would the close proximity to India affect them, what would happen if they chose to go back to America, could they cope with adapting to life back on the mainland? A host of deep, relevant questions. Many of them could not really be answered. You could only provide specifics and clarifications and the people would have to decide for themselves.

The people were really lost in a Bermuda triangle of confusion revolving around three main issues: the uncertainties regarding their future on The Nation of Good Hope, the deep hesitation they felt in leaving and going back to their old lives in America which somehow felt very strange after their yearlong experience on the floating landmass, and the fear and anxieties arising from their close proximity to gigantic India with its billion people and alien culture. Hari and Nilima struggled to help them navigate their way through this confusing jumble. Hari could answer any question on India, the social conditions, its politics, economy, the people, Hinduism, what it meant in everyday life, how other religions coexisted peacefully barring occasional minor disturbances, etc. Nilima, with her blend of American and Indian perspectives, addressed issues pertaining to what it meant to adapt to Indian conditions, where they would have difficulties, how they could anticipate and prepare for them, and so on. Where they could not help them at all was in telling them what future life on The Nation of Good Hope would be like. Kate's Government was still coping with large policy issues. They wanted to migrate to a socialistic free market economy, but to create the systems and structures to drive that was a gargantuan task. This is where a lot of people felt uncertain and anxious, quite understandably. But there was no way to address it. Only time would tell. This again would require a lot of faith and cooperation and the will to succeed, much as the situation had been when they were drifting aimlessly on the Pacific for a year. Hari and Nilima did their best, but it was not easy.

The volume of people coming for consultation increased so much that they could no longer meet with them individually. Instead they asked Father Duncan to make the main Church hall available for two hours in the morning and again in the afternoon. The hall could accommodate about three hundred people. Hari and Nilima would take questions from the people and answer them, encouraging the crowd to join in and voice their opinions. This led to an open exchange of views which was as helpful, if not more, than the information Hari and Nilima could provide. The two sessions became immensely popular. There really was a crying need for it and news about this fantastic service The Church of Good Hope was offering spread by word of mouth and people started coming by the thousands every day. There was no way they could accommodate all the people. Hari talked to Father Duncan about televising their show. They could have only one program a day and limit the live audience to about 150 so that the T.V. camera crew and their equipment could be accommodated. In addition to questions from the floor they would also take questions from people calling in. This would enable everyone on The Nation of Good Hope to take part without having to drive long distances. The idea appealed to Father Duncan. He persuaded KLAN to try a pilot program for a week. The program was called "Why worry? Ask Hari!" It aired from 10 a.m. to 12:00 p.m. every morning, including weekends. From the very first day the program became a huge hit. The ratings soared and by the end of the week Hari was a national celebrity. They addressed the same types of questions as before. Questions related to economy, social services, retirement, pension, health insurance and the like, which they could not address, they referred to Kate and her Cabinet. Kate or one of her Cabinet members would then come on the show and answer the questions to the best of their ability describing the policies either already in place, or being considered, how they would be implemented, when the people would actually see the changes, what the implications to the average citizen would be, and so on. This format proved very successful. The program met a real need of the people and went a long way in assuaging them and reassuring them that a superb team was in place working hard to address all the issues they were worried about. People who had entertained doubts began to feel much better, their confidence had been restored and they were fully behind Kate and the Cabinet willing to wait patiently to see how things would turn out.

One evening, Hari was having dinner with Kate in her house. They had been discussing the T.V. Community Service program and what a difference it had made. Kate had been thrilled with the positive changes she could see in peoples' attitudes.

"You and Nilima have done such a fantastic job, Hari. It has made life so much easier for me. Things are fast beginning to take shape and soon everyone will feel settled," she said.

"You are wrong, Kate," Hari shook his head, "things are far from settled. They are just beginning."

"What do you mean?" Kate asked.

"You know what I mean. Do you really believe that 10 million of you can hide behind an artificial barrier trying to isolate yourselves from a billion Indians? No way. Impossible. You could build a wall as high as you wish all along the border, but you still couldn't do it. Remember the Berlin wall?"

"But we don't want a wall. We don't want to isolate ourselves. We want to mix, interact, experience the spirituality of India."

"Any kind of long term interaction based on mutual trust and respect is only possible among equals Kate. If not, only one kind of interaction is possible: master and slave. Look at what happened to British rule. They were here for over three hundred years, but they had to leave. You have chosen to remain, you don't want to leave. That means you don't want the kind of interaction the British had with us, which means you have no choice but to assimilate, to merge with India."

"The thought has occurred to me Hari, but it is not so simple. Our people will resist. They have everything to lose and nothing to gain. They will think that I sold them out for personal reasons."

"Wrong again. They chose to stay back, didn't they? They chose a market free economy over a free market economy, didn't they?"

A characteristic, neat little turn of phrase from Hari summarizing something on which volumes could be written, Kate couldn't help admiring it silently in her own mind.

"The T.V. shows have made a tremendous difference, for sure," Hari continued, "Father Duncan has managed to instill an admiration for Indian spirituality and the Indian classics, in them. Surely, with a little exposure they'll appreciate Indian culture too. It is very deep Kate, Indian culture is very deep. It is too inward looking, that's its only problem and I'm hoping that's precisely what this interaction will cure. All this poverty, dirt, corruption, insanitary conditions, all superficial. Mere surface issues. A good, stable government can get rid of it in 10 years."

"Looks like you have given it a lot of thought, Hari. Do you have a plan?"

"Not so much a plan as wishful thinking. A plan would need your organizational skills. All I have is a sketchy outline. Here's what I have been thinking: hold a referendum proposing a merger. Suggest to your people that you can create a sort of a union territory under the protection of the Indian Government. People from all over India would be free to come and go as they please. So would your people. They can travel where they like. Tell them the territory of Good Hope will have a special status, more special than Kashmir. No Indian will be allowed to own property here, so they can keep it from becoming congested. You can maintain your own defense forces. Keep your special relationship with America. You get the picture."

"Yes, but what's in it for the Indian Government, why should they agree to this?"

"Are you kidding? Just this would be manna from heaven for them. They'll grab it for the sheer prestige and status it confers on them, not to mention the infinitely improved relations with America that is bound to follow. But that's not what I am thinking of. I am not suggesting that's how you should negotiate with the Indian Government. I am thinking of a much bigger role for you than that. The malaise that plagues India, I view you as the Good Witch from the North, who with a magical wave of her wand will rid India of its problems."

"Hey, hey, hey! hold on," interrupted Kate, "you are going too fast for me. Explain what exactly you have in mind."

"You should lay down terms and conditions for merger. Most important, India should change its constitution to create a federal structure like in America. Presidential form of government at the center with autonomy to the states. Privatize all public sector companies, invest heavily in infrastructure, clean air, clean water, good roads, telecommunications. Stop the incessant bickering with Pakistan. Get American help to resolve the Kashmir issue. In other words, get rid of the non-issues, so we can focus on the real issues. If we do this, I guarantee you that India will be on par with Europe in 10 years and catch up with America in 15. Now as far as you all are concerned, you must insist on getting dual citizenship - you are Indians and Good Hopers. Good Hopers? Is that the right term?"

he didn't wait for an answer. "Anyway, you should be guaranteed special status like I mentioned earlier. You must be allowed to vote and to create your own party and run for election at any level, including president. This is the crucial part," he stopped.

His plan was now dawning on Kate. "You call that a sketchy outline? That's a meticulous plan. That's all you've been doing when I am not here, right? Scheming and plotting," she was smiling.

"I am serious, Kate. This is the only way. If not, you might as well return to America right now. You cannot expect to experience Indian spirituality in half measure from behind a screen."

"Hari," said Kate, suddenly serious, "this a great plan in every way except one. It is not practical. There is no way the people will support it. You hear their concerns every day. Their concerns about India even outweighs their anxieties about the uncertainties facing The Nation of Good Hope. You talk to them every day, you know."

"But you are wrong, Kate. Yes, I do talk to them every day. I have a good feel for what they are thinking. You must try it out."

"No Hari, you are getting carried away with your idealism. Trust me, this will fail. And fail badly. It will trigger paranoia on a scale that will dwarf what we saw when we were drifting on the Pacific. May be we can revisit this in ten years, but definitely not now. We have to maintain a clean separation from India for the foreseeable future and let the people absorb Hinduism and Indian culture by osmosis. Sure, quite a few will want to cross the border and travel within India to see for themselves what it is like. And we should strongly encourage that. Promote it even. But we can't push for anything like a merger now. We have to maintain our sovereignty and remain separate." This was the first serious difference of opinion that had arisen between them since they met. Kate was discovering how tenacious Hari could be.

"But, why do you have to jump to that conclusion? Why can't you hold a referendum and let the people decide?" he insisted.

"Because, pubic opinion is a very fragile thing, Hari. People's mood swings are deeper and more frequent than a teenager's. If we lose them once, it will be very hard to get them back. That's why."

"Let's ask Father Duncan and see what he says. You told me yourself that he has a better feel for The Good Hopers' pulse than anyone else." Hari was pretty sure Father Duncan would support him.

But Hari was in for a surprise. When Kate and he met Father Duncan to have a private discussion on this subject, Father Duncan was in emphatic agreement with Kate. He made almost the same points Kate did. He was in full agreement with Hari's plan as a long term vision, but he too felt that the time was not ripe now for going ahead with it. Except for one thing. He thought the dual citizenship idea was excellent. If Kate and the Cabinet could negotiate a unilateral dual citizenship agreement with India, one which granted dual citizenship to Good Hopers but not to Indians, that would be a great way of easing the Good Hopers into the Indian environs. They could choose to participate in the Indian society, Government and politics when and how they wanted. They could remain within their cocoons on The Nation of Good Hope, or venture into India, to the degree they wanted and at the pace they wanted.

Both Kate and Hari were disappointed with this idea for opposite reasons. For Hari it was too little, for Kate it was still too much. She just didn't think people were ready for this. But she had too much respect for Father Duncan to reject his idea outright. In any event, a referendum had to be held soon to ascertain how many people wanted to go back to America and how many would choose to remain. They couldn't have four million undecided people. The logistics of evacuation was overwhelming as it is. Both here and on the American side. It was far greater on the American side. America had offered a very generous rehabilitation package to every returning family. They would cover the full costs of repatriation and arrange for housing and living expenses for a two year period, regardless of where in America they wanted to move to. They couldn't possibly keep such a generous policy open ended. The best President Walters could do was to get Congress to approve a five year window. The Good Hopers didn't have to decide right now, they had up to five years to decide. And of course, they would have dual citizenship forever. They could go back to America whenever they chose, except the rehabilitation program would expire in five years.

Kate met General Patterson to discuss the referendum to be conducted. She told him that she wanted to add unilateral dual citizenship with India to the referendum. General Patterson was aghast, "Kate, I am sorry, I have to disagree with you on this one. What's to be gained by having a dual citizenship agreement? You may call it unilateral or whatever, it can only mean one thing to the Indians, an

240

open invitation to stick their neck into our affairs. It will be like the story of the camel and the tent, if we allow them to stick their neck in here, then soon hundreds of millions of them will crowd around here and we'll move out, head back to America. I guarantee you, that's what's going to happen." All the time he was speaking, Kate was thinking, "How would he have reacted if I had shared Hari's full proposal with him? Probably immediately revoked Hari's temporary passport and forbidden him from ever setting foot on The Nation of Good Hope." As soon as he stopped she said aloud, "General, I don't think so. You have seen the effect Father Duncan's religious services and Hari and Nilima's Community Services have had on the people. They are thirsting for this. Believe me, everyone on this landmass has had a longer spiritual journey than a physical journey. That includes you and me. I've discussed this with Father Duncan and he strongly supports the idea. In any case, what's the harm? If people don't want it, we'll drop it. We are just asking them for their opinion, right?"

"You know very well, asking is the same as telling in this case. They'll wonder why it is even on the referendum. They'll think, if it's there then the President must want it. You know how people interpret things."

Even though Kate entertained similar misgivings, she remained firm, "No General, I disagree. This is a mature set of people, not some unseasoned easily impressionable bunch of people who can be swung one way or the other. Let's put it out and see what they feel." General Patterson agreed reluctantly.

Soon the referendum was conducted. On the issue of staying on The Nation of Good Hope vs., returning to America, of the four million previously undecided people, one million opted to go back. The remaining three decided to stay. The other two groups, those who had previously chosen to stay and those who had chosen to return, didn't change much. So a total of about three million people would return as soon as they could. The other nine million chose to join the experiment, much influenced by Father Duncan and Hari and encouraged by all the plans Kate's Government was putting in place. This was not very surprising, everyone had anticipated this. But what did surprise Kate was that almost 75% of the people polled voted in favor of a unilateral dual citizenship treaty with India. That was practically everyone who chose to stay back! They didn't just want to stay back, they wanted to explore and experience India. Kate was extremely surprised, she didn't think this idea would get the peoples' support. Neither Father Duncan nor Hari was surprised in the least.

The logistics of evacuation became a little simpler, but would still entail a tremendous amount of coordination and resources. Instead of the six million people they once had anticipated leaving, only three million had chosen to do so, but that was still an overwhelming number. It would take several months to complete, if everything went without a hitch.

After the referendum results were out, General Paterson requested a meeting with Kate. "Kate," General Paterson said, "I had already made my feelings known to you before the referendum. You can't transfer the burden of certain decisions to the public. They don't necessarily see things clearly. They get influenced by the transient mood of the time. And that's exactly what has happened. I too have beliefs of my own. It's one thing to embrace the spirituality of another country. But to open your borders to them. I can't stomach that. I like the way we are. I like what we have built here. Why couldn't we keep it that way? I am sorry, I can't be part of that. I'll be submitting my resignation. I plan to return to America with my family as soon as I can."

Kate begged him to reconsider. They were not going to open their borders to Indians, they would just make it easier for the Good Hopers to try India out in a deeper sense than would have otherwise been possible, she argued. It was no use. General Paterson was adamant. For the first time since their association, Kate and the General disagreed sharply. He had stood by Kate at every hour of crisis in the past year, giving her advice, confidence and strength. Kate felt very upset and sad. If he had so much opposition to dual citizenship, then how would Hari's proposal have fared, she wondered. She tried hard to make him change his mind. It was no use, General Patterson remained firm.

Kate began her negotiations with the Indian Government. A stunned Prime Minister Dalal had jumped for joy when he heard Kate's proposal of unilateral dual citizenship for The Good Hopers. He was smart enough to realize this meant a big boost to his career as the leader of India. He would now be a prominent international figure as well. He presented Kate's proposal with enthusiasm to his cabinet and to the Upper and Lower houses of Parliament. The Supreme Court was also consulted. Hari was right. The proposal got unanimous support, and the President of India, the figurehead under the existing constitutional framework, gave it the formal seal of approval. Most political leaders had seriously misjudged the situation. They dreamt of manipulating The Nation of Good Hope to their advantage and taking control of the abundant resources and advanced technology they had. Prime Minister Dalal had no such illusions, he had a much better idea of the stuff Kate was made of.

President Walters had not been very enthusiastic about the idea of a unilateral dual citizenship agreement with India. He had tried to dissuade Kate. But Kate had resisted. She had told President Walters that she and her people really believed that this was their destiny. President Walters was not convinced, but there wasn't much that he or anyone else could do to stop it as long as The Nation of Good Hope wanted it.

India and The Nation of Good Hope signed the unilateral dual citizenship agreement. Good Hopers could now move about India freely and to their hearts content.

CHAPTER 27

*A*nother year passed by. Much of the transformation Kate and her Cabinet had initiated had taken deep root, though much work still needed to be done. All of the nearly three million people who had chosen to return to America had been repatriated.

One morning, Father Duncan said to Hari, who had slept over, with a mischievous glint on his face, "How long do you propose to continue to trouble an old man?"

Hari was caught unawares, "I am sorry Father," he stuttered, "I didn't realize it was such an inconvenience."

"You have heard of the Presidential Mansion that is being built?" Father Duncan had broken into a broad grin. Somewhat belatedly Hari got his drift. In spite of Kate's opposition, the cabinet had approved the construction of a Presidential residence, both for reasons of security as well as national prestige. It was nearing completion and was expected to be inaugurated in a month or two.

"Of course Father, I have plans to move in," he said, also grinning.

"What are you waiting for then?" Father Duncan egged him on. The thought of proposing to Kate had been on Hari's mind. Father Duncan's gentle nudging had its effect. Feeling uncharacteristically shy, Hari had proposed to Kate. A blushing Kate had agreed.

When their wedding date was announced, Hari had said to Kate in jest, "Kate, you know you are a *kanyastree*, a married maiden. You were married before, which makes you a *stree*, Sanskrit for a married woman, but you are still a *kanya*, which means virgin, on Indian soil. I ensured that. Or have I?" He had winked and Kate had pinched him. "OK, so let's assume I have. That means you are a *kanyastree*. If *kanyakumari* is a tautology, then *kanyastree* is an oxymoron. And it's a well established fact that I am a moron. I can well imagine how the world press is going to report our wedding: 'Oxymoron weds moron'." Kate had pinched him again, harder.

Two weeks later Kate and Hari stood on the wedding platform, specially constructed on the Kanyakumari beach across from the temple of Kanyakumari. A huge crowd had gathered on the Kanyakumari beach to witness the ceremony which was being broadcast live by CNN to all corners of the world. An even larger crowd, as many of the nine million as could crowd into the narrow space, had gathered on the Good Hope side. People were packed close to each other on the beach, inside buildings, on the roads, wherever they could. It was the first practical proof that the landmass had stabilized, though no one thought of that. Everyone else who couldn't find room there was watching the ceremony live on T.V.

Among the many important guests who had assembled to witness the wedding were President Walters and Prime Minister Dalal. Hari had minutes ago tied the holy chain, at the auspicious moment, around Kate's neck, to symbolize their union. The wedding, witnessed by the fire God, represented an unbreakable seal according to Vedic rituals.

Kate and Hari stood next to each other, waving to the crowd, tired but happy. Hari had a smile on his face. He was thinking of his oxymoron gag. Kate looked much more serious. She was thinking how the wedding symbolized several unions on several planes. Of The Nation of Good Hope and India. Of East and West. Of Kanyakumari and Shiva. Of Kate and Hari.